THE ADVENTURES OF

4 STORIES

Printed in the United States of America
First Paperback Edition, January 2019
1 3 5 7 9 10 8 6 4 2

Library of Congress Control Number: 2018953272
ISBN 978-1-368-04576-6

For more Disney Press fun, visit www.disneybooks.com
Visit DisneyChannel.com

336140813685549

SUSTAINABLE
FORESTRY
INITIATIVE
Certified Chain of Custody
Promoting Sustainable Forestry
www.sfiprogram.org
SFI-01054
The SFI label applies to the text stock

THE ADVENTURES OF

4 STORIES

ADAPTED BY MARILYN EASTON

 PRESS

LOS ANGELES · NEW YORK

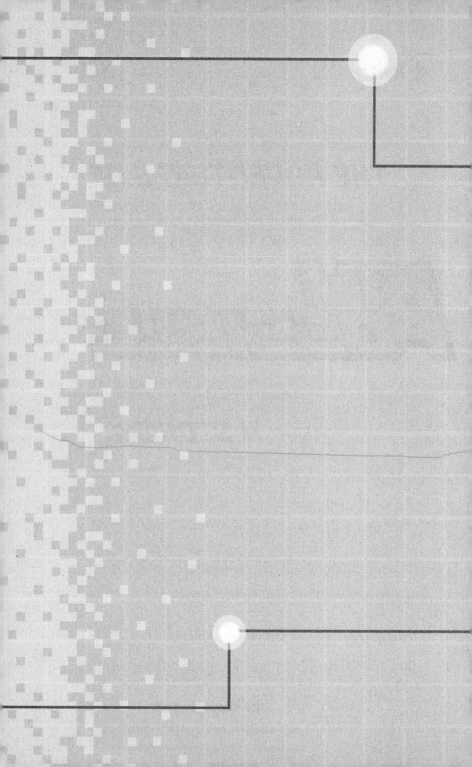

Notes for Mission #4140

Here's the sitch: Wade just got word that the evil Drakken—or Dr. Drakken as he likes to be called, even though he isn't <u>technically</u> a doctor—just broke out of prison <u>again</u>. The mad scientist and his mad sidekick, Shego, were last spotted in Alaska near the site of an oil rig that mysteriously disappeared. So Ron and I are off to the Last Frontier to stop whatever pure evilness they are up to. Unfortunately, I haven't had a moment to update my winter wardrobe, so I'm stuck wearing last season's red fleece jacket. Hopefully, I can escape without anyone noticing.

I guess all this crime fighting started a few years ago when I accidentally intercepted a distress call. I was done with my homework, so I answered it. Instead of normal teenage stuff like babysitting, or maybe walking dogs, I got messages from people all over the world asking for help—serious help. Fighting-sinister-bad-guys kind of help. Pretty soon I realized that I really <u>could</u> do anything. Now when I'm not in school or at after-school activities, I save lives and capture evil criminals. My most frequent bad-guy interactions are unfortunately with Drakken. Some may even call him my archnemesis.

If Drakken has a plan for this pipeline, it feels a little too small for his world-domination agenda. There've also been rumors that he's set up an evil lair somewhere in Wisconsin. But what do Alaska and Wisconsin have in common? Maybe I'll find out on this mission. . . . One thing is for sure: I have to stop whatever they're up to before it's too late.

Name:	Dr. Drakken
Wanted For:	Attempting to take over the world
Strength:	He mostly leaves the fighting to his evil sidekick, Shego
Weakness:	Will reveal his evil plan even if you don't ask for details
Last Seen:	Escaping a maximum-security prison

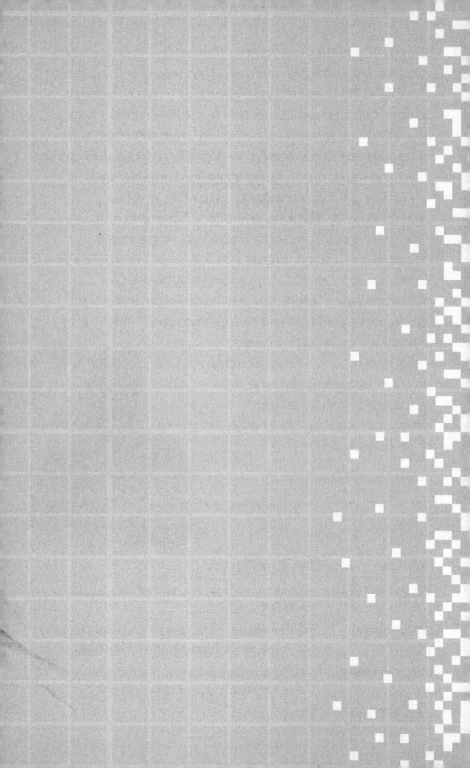

CHAPTER 1

"IT'S CRIMINAL!" Kim Possible cried.

Kim stared at an ugly baby-blue jacket on the screen of her Kimmunicator. The Kimmunicator was like a walkie-talkie combined with a high-speed computer. Kim wore it around her neck and used it to get information from all over the world—even the latest catalog from her favorite store, Club Banana.

Kim pushed a button to flip through the catalog. Different coats appeared on-screen. A boxy blue jacket with a zipper—*ugh*. A long wool overcoat—*as if*. A fluffy pink coat with big heart-shaped buttons. Kim wrinkled her nose in disgust.

"Someone at Club Banana is in major style denial," she said.

Just then, Kim spotted a green leather jacket

with a belt around the waist. The jacket matched Kim's green eyes perfectly.

"Now, *this* is me," she said. "Come to Kim."

Suddenly, the coat disappeared from the screen. Her friend Wade's face appeared instead.

"I have bad news," Wade told Kim.

Kim slumped in her beanbag chair. "No kidding," she said, pouting. "I *cannot* afford that jacket."

"I know," Wade said. "I looked at your bank account. You're broke. But that's not the bad news."

Wade ran Kim's website. He was a super genius. He was also super nosy.

"Apparently, the bad news is that my friend who runs my website has been hacking into my account," she said. Suddenly, a horrible thought crossed her mind. "Have you peeked at my diary?" she asked.

"Of course not," Wade said. "Anyway, the bad news is that your archfoe, Dr. Drakken, has escaped from prison."

A mug shot of Drakken, the mad scientist, flashed onto the screen. His face could have scared Frankenstein.

Drakken, as Kim knew, was pure evil. Drakken and his sidekick, Shego, were determined to take over the world. Kim had stopped them before. And it looked like she was going to have to stop them again.

Kim stared at Drakken's picture. Then a video appeared on the screen. She tapped the play button. It was a video of Drakken dancing, and it was totally embarrassing. Kim had seen enough.

"Drakken escaping from prison? That's major bad," she said.

"Almost as bad as last week at school—when you laughed so hard you squirted milk out of your nose," Wade said.

"Nobody saw that—" Kim started.

Suddenly, she gasped. "You *have* been reading my diary!"

"Good luck on the mission! Bye!" Wade said quickly. Before Kim could say another word, the Kimmunicator screen went blank.

CHAPTER 2

SPORTING A RED FLEECE JACKET, A HELMET, AND GOGGLES, KIM RACED ACROSS THE ALASKAN TUNDRA ON A DOGSLED. The huskies pulling the sled barked and panted as they charged through the snow.

Kim's best friend, Ron Stoppable, sat in the front of the sled. Ron was a tall, skinny boy with freckles. At the moment, his teeth were chattering from the freezing cold.

Akut, the large Alaskan man who owned the dogsled, sat behind Kim. He didn't seem bothered by the cold at all.

"Thanks for the lift, Akut," Kim said with a smile.

"No problem, Kim Possible. You saved my life. It's the least I can do to thank you," Akut replied.

"Oh, it was just an itty-bitty iceberg. So not the drama," Kim said.

"It's a beautiful day!" Akut added. "We don't get nice weather like this very often."

This is nice *weather?* Kim thought as snow stung her face. She was pretty sure even her eyelashes were frozen.

Suddenly, a shout came from the front of the sled. "Kim!" Ron cried. "I'm snow-blind!"

Kim casually reached forward and wiped the snow off Ron's goggles.

"Ron," she scolded, "you're supposed to be looking for signs of Drakken."

Earlier that day, an oil rig near the Alaskan pipeline had mysteriously disappeared. Kim thought Drakken might be behind it. She'd come to Alaska to look for clues.

As their sled got to the top of a hill, they saw a huge oil-drilling rig below them. Four helicopters hovered in the sky above it.

Ron pushed up his goggles. "Okay," he said, pointing. "That looks suspicious."

Kim rolled her eyes. "Thank you, Captain Obvious," she said. "Keep your eyes open for any—"

ROARRRRR! A loud engine drowned out Kim's

voice. A girl on a snowmobile flew over the top of the hill and raced up next to the dogsled. Her long black hair whipped in the wind.

"Shego!" Ron cried. "The mad scientist's mad sidekick."

Zipping past Kim and Ron's sled, Shego yelled, "Bye-bye!" She threw a handful of dog treats into the snow. The sled lurched to a halt as the huskies stopped to gobble up the treats.

Quickly, Kim clamped a snowboard onto her boots and chased after Shego.

"Thanks for the ride!" Kim said to Akut as she sped away.

Ron tried to put on his snowboard, but he lost his balance. He fell face-first into the snow. When he started to lift himself up, his hand grazed something in the shape of a bone. He grabbed the dog treat and brought it to his nose, inhaling deeply. He considered his options: it was a dog treat, but it could also be a delicious snack. He stuffed the treat into his mouth.

"*Mmm*," Ron said, chewing. "Bacon-y."

Meanwhile, Kim was racing down a steep slope. Shego was only a few feet ahead of her.

Now that she was closer, Kim noticed that Shego was wearing a leather jacket. It was just like the one she'd seen in the Club Banana catalog. Only Shego's was black.

"Nice jacket!" Kim called out. "Club Banana?"

"The very latest!" Shego shouted back proudly.

"Get a new lifestyle, Shego," Kim said. "Green is the new black."

Shego glared at Kim. "And this advice comes from a 'fashion don't' in fleece," she replied. Laughing, she stepped on the gas and zoomed away.

Kim looked down at her red fleece jacket. Fleece was perfectly acceptable in the snow, wasn't it? Then she scowled and raced after Shego.

The drilling rig was just ahead of them. But as Kim watched, the giant rig suddenly rose off the ground. The helicopters were lifting it into the air!

Shego slowed down for a second and turned to show Kim what she had in her hand—a bomb!

"It's going to blow the pipeline, Kimmy," said Shego. "I suggest you run away while you still can. Your skin definitely doesn't need more oil."

With a wicked laugh, Shego slapped the bomb

onto the front of her snowmobile. It only had twenty seconds until detonation. Then she drove the snowmobile straight at the oil pipeline.

Just as she reached the drilling rig, Shego leaped off the snowmobile. She grabbed the bottom of the oil rig as it rose into the air.

Then Shego was completely out of Kim's reach. As the rig flew higher, Kim spotted Drakken on it. He was waving at her mockingly. Then he started to do the dance she had seen in the video. It was still just as embarrassing.

On the ground, Kim tore after the snowmobile. The bomb was set to explode in five seconds. If it hit the pipeline, it would blow up half of Alaska!

When she was close enough, Kim took a flying leap off her snowboard. She landed on the snowmobile. Grabbing the handles, she steered the snowmobile away from the pipeline.

The snowmobile sped over a jump and soared through the air. At the last second, Kim leaped off. The snowmobile exploded in the air above her. Kim skidded to a stop at the edge of a cliff.

Stopping to catch her breath, Kim heard someone call her name.

"Here I come, KP!" Ron hollered. He slid down

the hill on his snowboard, his arms flailing wildly. He was totally out of control!

Kim knew what was coming next. She turned her head so she wouldn't have to watch.

Wham! Ron smacked into the metal pipeline.

Ooof! He fell back into the snow.

Kim looked up into the sky. The airborne drilling rig was a dot in the distance.

Drakken and Shego had escaped . . . for now.

CHAPTER 3

THE NEXT MORNING, KIM WOKE UP EARLY. She was feeling a little bummed about Drakken getting away, but she was really bummed that she couldn't afford the cool jacket she wanted. There had to be a way she could get it, so she gave herself a special assignment for the day. Mission: get the Club Banana jacket.

"Morning, Dad," Kim said as she sat down at the breakfast table. She set the Club Banana catalog next to her bowl of cereal.

Kim's dad, Dr. Possible, a rocket scientist, looked up from the blueprints he had laid out on the table. He was working on a design for a new rocket.

"Good morning," he said. "How's my teen hero?"

"Moderately bummed," Kim said. "Drakken got away."

"Well, I'm sure you'll get him next time," Kim's dad said absently. He turned back to his drawing, muttering, "Now these launch vectors are all wrong. . . ."

Kim slid the Club Banana catalog over her dad's rocket drawing. She pointed at the picture of the green leather jacket.

"Dad, what do you think of this jacket?" she asked. "For me. Just because."

Kim stuck her bottom lip out in an adorable pout. She looked at her father with puppy dog eyes.

Kim's dad looked at the jacket. Then he looked at the price of the jacket. He frowned.

"Cost-benefit ratio aside, Kimmy, don't you already have a functional coat?" he asked.

Kim stopped pouting and rolled her eyes. "It's a good thing fashion sense isn't genetic. My jacket's from *last season*," she told him. "It's *red*."

"Didn't you say red was the new black?" her dad asked.

"Red's dead, Dad," Kim said. Her father was *so* uncool. "*Green* is the new black."

Just then Jim and Tim, Kim's twin brothers, rushed into the room.

As usual, they're up to something, Kim thought.

"Dad!" they shouted in unison.

Kim glared at them. "Jim. Tim. I'm working here," she said.

Jim and Tim glared back. "So are we," Jim said.

"What's the combustion temperature of the J-200 fuel you developed?" Tim asked their father.

"Forty-seven degrees Celsius, Tim," Dr. Possible answered without missing a beat. "Why?"

Jim and Tim looked at each other nervously. "No special reason," said Jim.

Suddenly—*KABOOM!*—a loud explosion rocked the house.

"Gotta go!" Jim and Tim cried, dashing out of the room.

Ignoring the explosion, Kim's father turned his attention back to his daughter.

"You know, Kim," he said, "your problem reminds me of the time I asked for money for a new propulsion system. The university told me money doesn't grow on trees."

Kim sighed loudly. She put her head down on

the table. She'd heard this story, like, a million times before.

"I told them money is made of paper," Dr. Possible went on. "And paper comes from trees. So, in fact, money *does* grow on trees."

Kim looked up at her dad.

"And this relates to me how?" she asked.

"Not sure exactly," he said, scratching his head. "But no new jacket."

Kim's mom, Dr. Possible, a brain surgeon, walked into the kitchen. She was wearing her white doctor's coat and carrying a newspaper.

"Morning, Kimmy," she said. She kissed Kim's cheek. Then she noticed the Club Banana catalog. "Cute jacket," she said.

"Thank you!" Kim exclaimed happily. "Can you explain that to Dad, who incorrectly believes that I don't need it?"

"Sorry, baby. I'm due at the hospital," Kim's mom said. "But if you *need* it, I have a suggestion."

She held up a newspaper ad for Bueno Nacho, the local Mexican restaurant and one of Kim and Ron's favorite hangouts. Beneath the picture were big red letters that said "HELP WANTED."

"A job?" Kim stuck out her tongue. "At Bueno Nacho?"

"Now that's the way forward," her dad said cheerfully.

Kim slumped down in her seat, defeated. "You can't be serious," she said.

Her mom shrugged. "You practically live there anyway," she said.

Later, Ron and Kim were sitting in a booth at Bueno Nacho. As Kim filled out a job application, Ron munched on some nachos.

"Come on, Ron," Kim begged. "We practically live here anyway." She had finally come around.

"Kim, never work where you food," Ron said. He tossed a nacho chip into the air and caught it in his mouth.

Frustrated, Kim said, "It's the only way. The 'rents were totally not down for just buying me the jacket."

"Did you try the puppy dog pout?" Ron asked demonstrating.

"No effect," Kim said sadly. "If I want the jacket, I have to earn it."

"Harsh," said Ron. Then he picked up the nachos

and dumped them into a taco shell with melted cheese and extra sauce oozing out the sides.

Kim stared at the dripping mess. "What are you doing?" she asked.

"Taco meets nacho," Ron said proudly, displaying his handiwork to Kim. "I call it the tacho."

Kim looked at Ron with concern.

"Wait, wait, that's not it. Let me try again," Ron said. Then he paused for dramatic effect. "I call it . . . the naco."

"I call it gross beyond reason," Kim said with a look of disgust.

Ron took a huge bite of his naco. "You want some?" he asked with his mouth full.

Kim wrinkled her nose. Just then, two more customers walked into Bueno Nacho. They looked around and noticed Ron's loud crunching. With each bite he took, crumbs were flying everywhere. Then he took another delicious bite and let out a loud burp. The customers were still staring.

Kim smiled apologetically at the customers. Then she glared at Ron. "You know, we are dining at a restaurant. In public," she said.

"I mean, I wouldn't classify Bueno Nacho as a restaurant per se," Ron said matter-of-factly. "It's more of a food factory, a watering hole but for food, if you will."

"It's still a public space where some people would like to keep their appetites," Kim explained, trying not to laugh.

Ron looked at Kim. Then he looked at the other Bueno Nacho customers. He realized everyone was looking at him. Maybe he needed to tone down his naco enthusiasm a smidge.

"Okay, you may have a point," he said, lowering his naco for a moment.

Kim looked at the picture of the jacket in the Club Banana catalog.

"I did the math," she told Ron. "Two weeks of drudge work and I'm in green leather."

Kim was snapped out of her Club Banana fog when she suddenly heard someone calling her name.

"Miss Possible?" said a boy standing next to their booth.

Kim and Ron looked up. The boy was wearing a green-and-orange Bueno Nacho shirt and a necktie. He had greasy hair, freckly skin, and large glasses. He held a clipboard.

"I'm Ned, assistant manager here at Bueno

Nacho number five eighty-two," he said in a particularly whiny voice.

"Hola, amigo," Kim said. She gave him a big toothpaste-commercial smile.

Ned didn't smile back. "Your bilingual wiles will hold no sway with me, Miss Possible," he said. "I am management."

He picked up Kim's application and looked at it carefully. Ron made goofy faces behind his back.

Ned looked up. Ron stopped making faces just in time. He gave Ned a big smile.

"Is that a clip-on tie, Ned?" Ron asked brightly.

Ned nodded. "For quick removal in the event of a grease fire," he explained, popping the tie off and on to demonstrate. Then he turned to Kim and asked, "When can you start?"

"Born ready, sir," Kim replied enthusiastically.

Ned looked at another form. "And you?" he asked Ron.

"Me, what?" said Ron.

"Isn't this your application, Mr. Stoppable?" Ned asked. He held up a piece of paper.

Ron glared at Kim. "You didn't!" he cried.

Kim stuck out her bottom lip and looked at Ron with puppy dog eyes.

"It'll be more fun if we *both* work here," she said sweetly.

"Oh, no!" Ron cried, defeated. "Not the puppy dog pout!"

Kim smiled. Her parents might be immune to it, but it got Ron every time. It looked like Bueno Nacho had *two* new employees.

CHAPTER 4

THAT AFTERNOON, KIM AND RON STOOD BEHIND THE COUNTER AT BUENO NACHO LOOKING STUNNED. They wore stiff green-and-white polyester shirts and Bueno Nacho baseball caps. The smell of fried cheese and taco seasoning filled the thick air.

Ned handed each of them a large notebook. "Bueno Nacho SOP," he said.

"Excuse me?" Kim asked, weighed down by the stack of papers.

"Standard operating procedures," Ned explained as though Kim should already know that. "Learn them. Know them. Live them."

Ron shot Kim a dirty look. He leaned in closer and growled, "I'm going to get you for this."

Kim closed her eyes and pretended she couldn't hear him. "Two weeks to jacket . . . two weeks to jacket," she sang as she did a little dance.

Ned wasted no time getting his new employees trained. Their first lesson was the combo plate. As Kim plopped refried beans and squeezed salsa out of a ketchup bottle onto a paper plate, Ned watched over her shoulder.

"Not enough lettuce. Too much salsa," he snapped. "And don't get me started on those beans."

He pointed at Ron's plate. "Notice how he sculpts the frijoles, evoking the majesty of a Mayan temple," Ned said in a complimentary tone.

Happily surprised, Ron said, "Really? Ya think?" He admired his beans, which really *did* look sort of like a Mayan temple.

Ned placed his hand on Ron's back. "You're ready for burrito folding," Ned told him.

"Right on," Ron said proudly.

At the burrito counter, Ron swiftly folded beans and cheese into a perfect airtight package. He held it up to show Ned.

Ned smiled approvingly and made a note on his clipboard. Then he turned to Kim.

Kim held up her burrito for inspection, but the

end came unfolded. Beans and cheese oozed onto the counter.

Ned gave her a disappointed look.

"Possible, I'm putting you on cheese duty," he said. "Even *you* can push a button."

Ned led Kim over to a green machine with an image of melted cheese on it. He pushed a button, which also happened to be the only button on the machine. Liquid cheese squirted over a pile of tortilla chips.

Ned held the cheesy chips under Kim's nose.

"Meet the Cheese Machine 3000. So easy, there's only one button. Think you can handle this?" he asked.

"Mission: possible," she said with a defeated sigh.

As Ned walked away, Kim ripped the picture of her jacket out of the Club Banana catalog and taped it to the Cheese Machine 3000.

"I can get through this," she told herself. "Two weeks to jacket . . . two weeks to jacket . . ."

Suddenly, Kim's Kimmunicator beeped.

"What up, Wade?" she asked, tapping it and watching the hologram glow to life.

"I've scanned all recent satellite photos," he said

as he sipped his soda. "But there's no sign of the stolen laser drill."

Kim frowned. "It must be hidden," she said.

Suddenly, a shadow fell across the Kimmunicator's hologram. Kim looked up. Ned stood before her, looking unhappy.

"Playing video games on the job is not SOP," he whined. "I'm docking your pay an hour."

So unfair, Kim thought. *Try to do the world a favor and get docked an hour's pay.* Now she had two weeks *and* one hour until she could buy her jacket.

On the other side of the room, Ron was single-handedly running both the burrito station and the taco salad station. With one hand, he expertly placed lettuce in taco shells. With the other, he folded burritos into origami masterpieces.

"Multitasking?" Ned asked. "Excellent, Stoppable."

"Just doing my job, Ned," said Ron.

As Ned walked off to inspect the deep fryer, Kim shot a look at Ron.

"Hello? Kim to Ron!" she cried as she waved her hand in front of her friend's face. "You didn't even *want* this job!"

"I didn't know what I wanted, Kim," Ron said,

looking off into space. "I was lost. Adrift in the wilderness. But that was then," he said dramatically.

Ron leaned closer to Kim. There were tears in his eyes.

"Now I belong," Ron said, clutching his hand to his heart. A tear rolled down his cheek. "I belong to Bueno Nacho!"

Whirling around, Ron strode over to the door. He threw it open and hollered out to the world.

"Te amo este lugar!" he shouted with a fist in the air. "I love this place!"

CHAPTER 5

BUENO NACHO HAD NEVER SEEN AN EMPLOYEE LIKE RON. He worked like a machine, scooping beans, squirting hot sauce, and wrapping burritos. His perfect combo plates didn't have so much as a stray drip of salsa.

Ron enjoyed adding personal little touches to his tasks. "Fifty-eight, your order's great," he sang into the microphone. "Fifty-nine, lookin' fine. Sixty . . . uh, your order's ready."

Standing at the cheese machine, Kim was steaming. They'd only been working for two days, and already Ron had turned into some kind of Bueno maniac.

Suddenly, her Kimmunicator beeped. Kim tapped it and Wade appeared on the hologram screen.

"Go, Wade," she said.

"Check this out," Wade said, slurping soda from a supersize takeout cup. "Highly unusual—"

Suddenly, Ron swiped the screen and shut down the Kimmunicator. The screen went blank.

"What are you doing?" Kim asked.

Ron rapped his knuckles on the Cheese Machine 3000. "Ixnay on the Kimmunicator," he said, crossing his arms. "The nacho cheese needs some love."

Kim was at a loss for words. What was going on with Ron?

"Ron, we might have a lead on Drakken," Kim said. "Drakken . . . nachos . . ." Kim held up her hands as if she were a scale weighing the two sides. "I'm gonna have to go with Drakken."

"Well," Ron snapped uncharacteristically, "that kind of 'tude is narrowing the race for Employee of the Month."

Kim stared at him in disbelief.

"The race is between *you* and *you*," she snapped back.

Ron huffed angrily and turned his back to Kim. Kim huffed angrily and turned her back to Ron.

"Sometimes I feel like I don't even know you anymore," they said at the same time.

They turned and glared at each other. Not having anything more to say, they both stomped off.

As Ron walked away, Kim pushed the button on the Cheese Machine 3000. Cheese oozed over a pile of chips. She sighed. Kim pressed her Kimmunicator. "Wade, I need some assistance over here," she said.

"Sure, Kim. But first I was saying—" Wade responded.

"Sorry, Wade, we have to hold on that for now. I'm in a bit of a cheesy situation. Can you do a quick search on the Cheese Machine 3000 and pull up the operating manual? I need to find a way to shift this machine into auto-dispensing mode."

"Sure thing," Wade replied as the operating manual for the Cheese Machine 3000 popped up on the Kimmunicator screen.

"Perfect," said Kim as she started searching through the manual. *Bingo!*

She found just the information she needed. Kim began unscrewing the sides of the machine. This was definitely in direct violation of the Bueno Nacho standard operating procedures.

Once she had hacked the machine, Kim had

to make sure it was going to work. She placed a tray of nachos near the machine. The machine's arm grabbed the nachos, placing it under the cheese nozzle, and cheese began to ooze out. Kim inspected the tortilla chip. It was perfectly covered in cheese. She took a bite. It was delicious.

With her cheese-dispensing duties taken care of, Kim re-engaged with her Kimmunicator.

"Sorry, Wade," she said. "Now, you were saying there's something highly unusual?"

"Seismic activity . . . in Wisconsin," Wade told her.

A map of the United States appeared on the Kimmunicator screen. Red circles indicating an earthquake radiated from the state of Wisconsin.

"Quake in the Midwest?" Kim asked, slightly confused. "Major red flag."

"It gets weirder," Wade told her. "The epicenter is the world's biggest cheese wheel."

Kim stared at the map. Suddenly, she had an idea.

"Let me try something," she told Wade. Kim quickly punched the keys on the screen, searching through police files from the Midwest.

"Police report from the Cheese Wheel Mall shows a break-in at the Club Banana store," she reported back to Wade.

Wade shook his head. "I don't get the connection," he said.

"Only one thing was stolen," Kim explained. "A black leather jacket."

Kim's brow furrowed as she put the pieces together.

"Shego," she murmured.

Clicking off the Kimmunicator, Kim hurried over to Ned.

"Ned, I've gotta switch shifts," she said. "Something suddenly came up."

"Whatever," Ned said glumly.

Kim eyed him suspiciously. Where was the work responsibility talk she expected? "What's with you?" she asked.

"Go ask your new boss," Ned replied, jerking his thumb toward Ron.

"New boss?" Kim asked, surprised. Suddenly, Kim realized that Ron was wearing a green-and-orange Bueno Nacho assistant manager's shirt—with a clip-on tie!

Kim approached Ron and gave him a look.

"Corporate loved the naco," Ron explained, tugging on his new tie.

"Oh, really?" Kim said.

"They see big things in my future," Ron said, grinning smugly as he straightened his tie.

"Good for you," said Kim matter-of-factly. "Now let's go. Drakken's in Wisconsin."

Ron hesitated. "B-but your shift isn't over," he said.

"Ron," Kim said angrily, "an evil mastermind is in the Dairy State with a giant laser drill. I'm going. And I was hoping you'd come with me."

Ron glared at Kim. Their faces were inches apart.

"To be your *sidekick*?" he asked. "That's what this is all about, isn't it? You just can't stand that I'm better than you at something."

Kim couldn't believe what she was hearing. "You wouldn't even have this job if I didn't fill out your application!" she yelled.

"Kim, we could argue all day, but that's not gonna get this floor mopped," Ron said, pointing to a bucket and mop in the corner.

Kim had had enough. She grabbed the mop and shoved it into Ron's hands.

"Mop it yourself, *boss*," she said furiously. She jumped over the counter and strode toward the door. "And find yourself a new nacho drone. I quit," she said, storming out of the restaurant.

"Yeah? Well, find a new sidekick!" Ron yelled at the closed door.

Of course, Ned was close by and overheard everything.

"What are you looking at?" Ron asked him. He shoved the mop into Ned's hands. "I want that floor to sparkle!"

CHAPTER 6

KIM NEEDED TO STOP HOME AND GRAB SOME SUPPLIES BEFORE HER MISSION IN THE DAIRY STATE. While she was packing, she called her mom. She needed some reassurance after her argument with Ron.

"Mom, I just had a fight with Ron," Kim said into her phone. "He was all high-horse cause I bailed on work. And I really need to stop Drakken. But Ron thinks I quit because I can't take him being good at something, which would be really pathetic."

"I need a suture here," Kim's mom interrupted.

Then Kim noticed a beeping in the background. "Mom, do you have me on speaker?"

"Sorry, honey, I've got both hands in a sixty-two-year-old male's temporal lobe," Kim's mom replied as she turned on the operating saw. "Gotta go, honey. See you at dinner. Dad's picking up nacos!"

Soon Kim sat in the passenger seat of a crop-dusting plane. Her red hair flapped beneath her aviator cap as she soared over Wisconsin. She had gotten a ride from a crop-dusting pilot she had helped in the past.

"I can't tell you how much I appreciate this, Mr. Parker!" Kim yelled over the noise of the plane.

"After the way you saved my crop-dusting business, I'm only too happy to help!" he replied.

"No big, going organic was a no-brainer," Kim replied.

"Get ready!" the pilot shouted. "Now!"

The plane rolled over, and Kim dropped from her seat. Hundreds of feet above the ground, she yanked the cord on her purple parachute. The chute opened and Kim glided down to earth gracefully.

She landed on top of the biggest wheel of Swiss cheese she had ever seen. It was at least seven stories high and as wide as a city block. A small wedge was cut out of one side. A little monorail tram ran all the way around the giant wheel.

Kim sniffed at the surface and pulled off a chunk of cheese.

"Weird," she said. "A cheese-covered building." Just then, she heard the monorail approaching.

"Many people assume that this is a cheese-covered building," a tour guide announced to the group of tourists riding the monorail.

Kim ducked into one of the Swiss cheese holes and listened.

"In fact," the tour guide continued, "this marvel of dairy product architecture is one hundred percent pure Wisconsin Swiss."

"Ooooh!" the tourists said in unison.

The monorail passed by a slice that had been taken out of the cheese wheel.

"Oh, hey, look! Who cut the cheese?" the tour guide joked.

As the monorail passed, Kim suddenly realized that the cheese hole she was hiding in was actually a tunnel! She followed the tunnel, crawling deeper and deeper into the center of the giant cheese.

At last, she saw an opening. Kim crept to the edge and peered out.

The tunnel opened into a giant cavern hidden deep within the cheese wheel. Hundreds of feet below on the cavern floor, Kim saw Drakken's oil-drilling rig and several henchmen. She had found his secret lair!

Kim looked around, somehow impressed by his choice of location. "Okay, points for a bizarre hiding place," she murmured to herself. She ducked back into the cheese and called Wade.

"Wade, get this," she whispered into her Kimmunicator. "I'm inside the cheese wheel."

"Which, surprisingly, is not a cheese-covered building," Wade said knowingly. "It's one hundred percent pure Wisconsin Swiss."

"So I've heard," Kim replied. "Drakken's got the whole mad scientist's lair thing here. You know how they love the high ceilings."

"Kim, look in your pack," Wade said, taking a sip of his soda on the hologram screen.

Kim dug into her backpack and pulled out a red hair dryer.

"A hair dryer?" she asked, confused. "I'm more of a towel-off type."

"It only *looks* like a hair dryer," said Wade.

Kim flipped the power switch. Instantly, a shiny grappling hook popped out from the nozzle of the dryer.

Kim grinned. "You rock, Wade," she said, tapping her Kimmunicator to minimize the hologram.

Aiming high on the wall of the cavern, Kim fired the hook. *Thwack!* The steel hook plunged deep into the cheese. Quickly, Kim climbed down the wall. It was quite a long way down.

Once on the cavern floor, Kim tried to stay out of sight. Hearing Drakken, she ducked behind a large crate.

"Increase the drill's power!" Drakken shouted. "I want to reach that magma!"

Kim was just about to sneak out when she heard someone say, "Welcome, Kimmy."

Kim spun around. There stood Shego, wearing the Club Banana jacket. On either side of her stood two huge henchmen carrying laser weapons.

"May I take your coat?" Shego purred.

"You already did," Kim said. "Don't worry. It'll look better on me."

Springing forward, Kim knocked Shego to the ground. The henchmen rushed at her from either side, but Kim kicked her legs out in a wide split, knocking them both to the ground. She somersaulted forward, overthrowing a third henchman. Scrambling to her feet, she turned to run.

But ten more henchmen blocked her path. She spun around, looking for another way out. But Shego and the other henchmen were behind her. She was trapped!

Shego smiled. Her dark eyes gleamed.

"Face it, pumpkin," she said. "Fashion isn't the only thing in which I'm a step ahead."

As Kim glared at her, the henchmen closed in.

CHAPTER 7

KIM STRUGGLED, BUT IT WAS NO USE. The henchmen held her tight. They drove her up against a giant slab of metal.

Shego pushed a button. *Clank! Clank!* Iron shackles emerged from the metal slab. They clamped around Kim's wrists and ankles.

"Comfy?" Shego asked sarcastically.

Kim gave her a look. "Not particularly," she said.

"Good," Shego said with an evil smile.

Suddenly, a trapdoor opened right in front of Kim. Drakken rose up from the floor.

"Well, well," he said, chuckling. "Kim Possible. How nice to see you again. Especially now that you're helpless to stop me."

Rubbing his hands together excitedly, Drakken

leaned in close to Kim. "Shall I tell you my plan?" he asked. "It's quite impressive."

Kim wrinkled her nose. Drakken's breath was terrible.

Without missing a beat, Kim said, "You're using the world's most powerful laser drill to tap into the molten magma deep beneath the earth's crust."

Drakken blinked, annoyed. Kim had foiled his chance to reveal his evil plot. He was speechless for a moment.

"Ah!" he cried at last. "That's phase one. In phase two, which you did not guess, my Magmamachine will melt the entire state of Wisconsin. Which I will then rebuild and rename Drakkenville!"

"You're so conceited," Kim said, shrugging him off.

Drakken smiled. "I'll take that as a compliment," he replied.

Then he impatiently walked over to the laser drill and shouted, "Shego! How long?"

High up in the cab of the drill, Shego was working the controls. She looked at a gauge showing a graphic readout of the drill's descent through the earth's crust. It had nearly reached the magma.

"The alarm will go off when we hit magma," she said.

"You see?" Drakken crowed to Kim. "Any second now I will strike swiftly and without mercy."

"Actually," Shego called out, "make it more like half an hour to forty-five minutes."

Drakken scowled. "Fine. Whatever," he said, annoyed. "In roughly thirty to forty-five minutes, Wisconsin will be a smoldering memory, and the kingdom of Drakkenville will be born!"

He reached out and squeezed Kim's cheeks. "Say it with me—Drak-ken-ville." Drakken cackled evilly. "Doesn't that have a nice ring to it?"

CHAPTER 8

STANDING BY THE DRIVE-THROUGH WINDOW, RON SHOUTED OVER TO NED, "STEP IT UP! These customers have been waiting for over thirty seconds." He held up a stopwatch. "Thirty-three! Thirty-four!" he counted. *"Ándale!"*

Ned finished stuffing tacos into a paper bag. He hurried over to the drive-through window and handed the bag to a waiting customer.

"Have a *muy bueno* day," Ned said unenthusiastically. He turned around to find Ron holding a mop toward him. He grabbed the mop and sulked off.

Just then Ron heard a voice on the drive-through headset he was wearing.

"Ron!" the voice said.

"Welcome to Bueno Nacho," Ron said into the headset. "May I take your order?"

"Ron, it's *Wade*."

"Wade?" Ron said in surprise.

Ron stuck his head out the drive-through window. Wade was nowhere in sight.

"Where are you?" he asked.

"Not important," Wade told him. "Kim's in trouble. She found Drakken inside a giant cheese wheel. But I lost contact with her. She needs help. *Your* help."

"Well, well, well," Ron heard someone say in his other ear.

He turned. Ned was standing right behind him. He had heard everything.

"Looks like you've got a choice to make, Stoppable," Ned snarled. "What's more important? Your sacred duty as assistant manager? Or your pathetic role as goofy sidekick?"

Ned's eyes narrowed. Ron's lip curled back from his teeth.

"Well," Ron said at last, "that's no choice at all. I guess it's time to say *buenos noches*, Bueno Nacho."

Ron leaped over the counter and rushed out the door to save Kim.

A short time later, Ron was in Wisconsin, riding the cheese wheel monorail with the other tourists.

"Question!" Ron called out to the tour guide. "Is this some kind of cheese-covered building?"

The tour guide chuckled. "You know, you'd be surprised at how many people think that," she said.

Inside Drakken's lair, Kim was still pinned to the metal slab. Drakken laughed as she struggled against the iron shackles.

"Don't bother," he sneered. "The Midwest is about to receive a molten calling card from a certain Dr. Drakken."

Drakken looked up at the drill's cab, where Shego was still busy at the controls.

"Shego!" he shouted. "I'm waiting."

"So, read a magazine," Shego snapped. "I'm working."

"Excuse me," he said to Kim. "I have to go make

a scene." Scowling fiercely, he marched up to the cab.

"Can't you drill any faster?" he shouted at Shego. "I've built an entire army of evil robots in the time it's taking you to break through the earth's crust!"

Just then, Ron made his way into the cheese and tiptoed around the laser drill. He crept up to Kim.

"Ron!" she whispered happily.

"Everything's okay, Kim," he said. "I'm here to save the day!"

But before he could make a move, Ron was grabbed from behind by two henchmen. They turned him around to face Shego. She looked at his Bueno Nacho uniform with disgust.

"Is that a clip-on tie?" she asked.

Ron's face turned red.

"Heh, heh, heh," he laughed nervously. He popped off the tie as Drakken's henchmen shackled him next to Kim.

CHAPTER 9

"GUESS THAT WASN'T MUCH OF A RESCUE PLAN," RON ADMITTED.

"Not as great as your Bueno Nacho bathroom-break chart," Kim replied, annoyed.

Ron looked at her sheepishly. "I went a bit over-board with assistant manager power. You were right," he said.

Kim hung her head. She didn't want to have to say it but felt she had to. "I did resent your superior burrito technique," she admitted. "You're entitled to excel. Forgive me?"

"Duh, of course," said Ron. "Forgive me?"

Kim grinned. She could never stay mad at Ron. "Totally," she said.

Just then, a dark shadow fell over them. Drakken had returned!

"Awww . . . that's so sweet," the mad scientist said mockingly. "Friends again. Just in time to be fried in magma!"

Ron gulped and looked at Kim.

"Remind me again why I rushed over?" he said.

At that moment, the drill's beam cut through the last layer of the earth's crust. It splashed into a sea of molten rock.

"The drill's into the magma!" Shego cried out to Drakken.

"About time!" he said. "Activate the Magmamachine!"

Shego hit a few buttons on the control panel. The laser beam shut down. Slowly, the giant laser drill moved to the side of the cavern.

In its place, a monstrous machine moved over to the hole. Kim and Ron watched in horror as one end of the machine slammed down over the magma hole. It looked like the oil rig Drakken had stolen from Alaska, but it had some new parts added to it.

"That would be so cool if it weren't going to hurt us," Ron whimpered.

"Showtime!" Drakken roared, smiling at last. "Deploy the barrel and activate the magma pump!"

One of his henchmen turned a dial on the control panel. The top of the machine opened and a huge, telescoping barrel shot upward. It grew longer and longer until it punched through the top of the cheese wheel!

Chunks of Swiss flew into the air. More rained down around the monorail, frightening tourists.

Deep inside the cheese wheel, the Magmamachine began to suck magma from the center of the earth. Kim gasped. In only a few minutes, the cannon would spray fiery magma over the entire state of Wisconsin. They were almost out of time!

Yawning sleepily, Ron started to nod off.

"Ron!" Kim whispered loudly. "Ron! Wake up! This is no time for a nap."

"What? Oh, sorry, my extra shifts at Bueno Nacho have been really draining," Ron started to explain.

"We need a plan," Kim interrupted. She motioned toward the button that activated the shackles. "We need to push that button to release the shackles."

Ron looked down. He noticed a mop lying against

the wall, just out of reach. If he could knock over the mop, they might have a chance. He reached his leg out. He tried once . . . twice . . . and *bam!* The mop fell over and rolled to Ron's feet.

"It looks like my Bueno Nacho training has real-life applications, as well," Ron said. He placed his foot expertly on the tip of the mop handle. He applied pressure, and the mop shot up, knocking against the button.

The shackles released. Kim and Ron fell to the floor. Quick as a wink, they scrambled to their feet and dashed away.

CHAPTER 10

RON AND KIM CREPT AROUND THE BASE OF THE GIANT LASER DRILL, LOOKING FOR A WAY TO STOP THE MAGMAMACHINE. Drakken and Shego were busy aiming the machine's cannon at Milwaukee. They didn't notice that Kim and Ron were free.

"Ron! Get to the laser drill," Kim said. "I'll take care of Shego."

"Great plan!" said Ron.

He took one step. Then he stopped and looked back at Kim.

"What exactly is the plan again?" he asked.

"Ron, you're the genius who invented the naco," Kim said. "You've got a building made of cheese here. Get creative."

Ron grinned.

"It will be my masterpiece," he said.

"Be careful!" Kim and Ron said at the same time.

"Jinx, you owe me a soda," Kim said. She winked and dashed away.

Just then, Drakken glimpsed her out of the corner of his eye. He turned and saw the empty shackles.

"They've escaped!" Drakken cried.

"No. Really?" Shego said sarcastically.

"The buffoon is nothing," Drakken said as Shego started after them. "Find Kim Possible!"

Quickly, Kim leaped up a stack of crates. At the top, she stopped to catch her breath. Suddenly, Shego soared over Kim's head. She landed in front of Kim. Her hands crackled with green electricity.

"Lesson time, princess," Shego hissed.

"With that trendy coat weighing you down? I'm thinking not," Kim said.

Shego lunged at Kim with a flying kick. Kim tumbled out of the way at the last second. Shego flew past her and landed on her feet. She whirled around and went at Kim again. Kim ducked and spun, blocking Shego's blows with martial arts moves.

Shego was furious. With a fierce growl, she lunged forward and threw a mighty punch.

Kim stepped out of the way. Shego's hand smashed through a wooden crate.

She spun and faced Kim again, her eyes glowing with anger.

Meanwhile, Drakken was at the controls of the Magmamachine.

"Here comes the magma!" he cried, cackling evilly. He didn't notice Ron climbing the ladder to the laser drill's cab.

Ron pulled the cab door shut behind him. He stared at the blinking lights, keys, and dials on the drill's control panel. There were a lot of buttons. *This is a precision instrument. Incredibly complex,* Ron thought. He paused for a moment. *Better mess with everything,* he decided. He began pushing all the buttons and twisting all the dials.

Lights flashed on and off. An alarm shrieked.

"Stop him!" Drakken screamed.

A group of henchmen ran toward the drill.

In the cab, Ron squinted at the label next to a large lever.

"'Angle adjustment'?" he read. Shrugging, Ron pushed the lever forward.

The laser cannon tilted up and hit the henchmen. They tumbled every which way.

"Booyah!" Ron cried, pumping his fist in the air.

As the laser beam hit the cavern wall, the cheese began to melt. Slowly, the laser swiveled around. The entire building started to collapse. Gooey, fondue-y cheese flooded the floor of the cavern.

The beam was heading straight for the crate where Kim and Shego were still fighting. Kim looked up just in time. Quickly, she grabbed her hair dryer and fired the grappling hook into the ceiling. Kim leaped. A second later, the laser blasted the wooden crate to bits.

"Ahhh!" Shego screamed. She tumbled through the air and landed in a river of melted Swiss.

Kim swung through the air on the end of her rope. Below her, she saw Ron standing on top of the laser drill, which was almost submerged in melted cheese. She swooped down and grabbed him just before the drill sank into the gooey mess.

Drakken was too busy watching his Magmamachine fill up to notice what was going on. At last, it was full. The lights on the control panel turned green.

"Eat magma, Milwaukee!" Drakken yelled. He slammed his fist down on the fire button. But nothing happened.

"Why isn't Milwaukee eating magma?" Drakken asked, confused.

He hit the button again and again. But it was no use. The Magmamachine was completely clogged with melted Swiss.

Drakken looked down. Cheese was rising around his legs.

"Please, do not tell me that this place is actually made of cheese!" he cried. *"I thought it was a cheese-covered building!"*

"Oh, golly, no," said the tour guide, who floated by on a crate. "You'd be surprised by—" *Gloop.* Before she could finish, a big cheese wave covered her.

Drakken frantically worked the controls but with no luck. Suddenly, he was sucked into the river of melted cheese.

High above, Kim and Ron climbed into a hole in the wall. They crawled out the other side just in time.

As the cheese wheel collapsed behind them, they heard Drakken scream, "This is not over, Kim Possible!"

And then he was swept away in a current of melted Swiss.

CHAPTER 11

"DRAKKEN'S PLAN IS SO FOILED!"
Kim said.

"Oh, it's over," Ron agreed. "I call it bad guy *con queso.*"

He stepped back to admire his handiwork. The cheese had cooled off quickly. The cheese wheel looked more like a squashed cheesecake. Drakken, Shego, and the henchmen were all stuck in the hardened cheese.

Later, Ron and Kim were back in their usual spot at Bueno Nacho—in a booth. Ron munched a naco. Kim sipped a soda and sighed sadly.

"What's wrong, KP?" Ron asked. "We won."

"I'm very happy," Kim said. "Really."

"You don't *sound* happy," said Ron.

"Okay," Kim said. "I know this is beyond shallow, but I saved the world, and I'm no closer to owning that Club Banana jacket."

She put her chin in her hand and pouted. "Maybe," Ron said. "Maybe not."

He reached under the table and pulled out a box. The Club Banana logo was printed on the top.

"Ron?" Kim squealed. She had the best friend in the world! She tore open the box and pulled out the green leather jacket.

Kim held it up. Her green eyes twinkled.

"It's no big deal," Ron said modestly. "My naco bonus was *muy bueno*."

"You are *too* sweet," she said, hugging the jacket. "I love it!"

Just then, Ned walked up to their table. He had gotten his assistant manager job back. He had on his old green-and-orange shirt and regulation clip-on tie.

And over that, he was wearing a green leather Club Banana jacket.

"What are you wearing?" asked Ron.

Ned held up a Club Banana catalog picture.

"Somebody left this picture over the cheese machine," he said. "I just *had* to have it." He turned up the collar on his new coat. "*Viva* me!" he exclaimed.

Ron and Kim looked at each other. Then they looked at Kim's new coat.

"Exchange it?" Ron asked.

"Oh, yeah," Kim said as she threw the jacket back into the box and put the top on tightly.

Wear the same jacket as Ned? As if!

THE CHEESY DETAILS

Local News for Cheeseheads

SWISS CHEESE BUILDING TURNS TO FONDUE

The great state of Wisconsin was rocked yesterday by the destruction of the world's largest cheese wheel and favorite local tourist attraction. All that's left of the cherished location is a melted pile of delicious cheese.

Several reliable sources revealed that the structure was not a cheese-covered building as commonly believed but, rather, a building made entirely of 100 percent pure Wisconsin Swiss, considered by many to be a marvel of dairy product architecture.

The Wisconsin Swiss Cheese Association (WSCA) has begun planning a replacement building. Jack Monterey, president of the WSCA, confirmed that the new construction will be a cheese-covered building, to prevent future similar catastrophes.

Meanwhile, in Alaska, a major oil rig vanished into thin air. Local dogsledder and iceberg activist Akut said, "How could a major oil rig just vanish into thin air? It's not like it's made entirely out of cheese or anything." Local authorities have declined to comment, but our keen reporter instincts tell us the replacement oil rig will likely not be made entirely out of cheese.

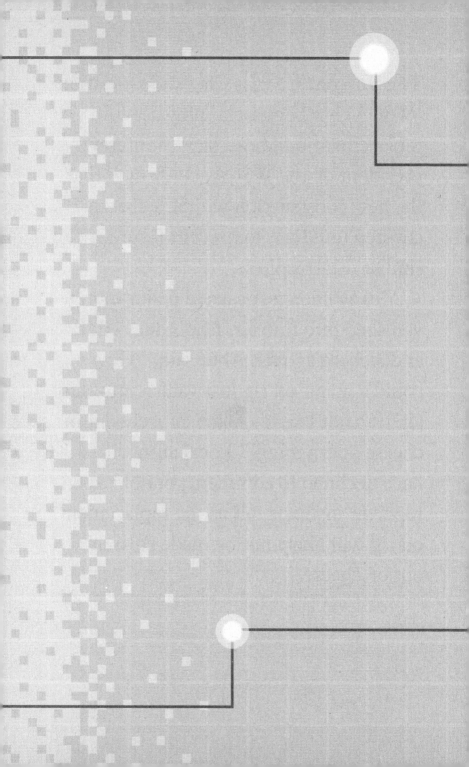

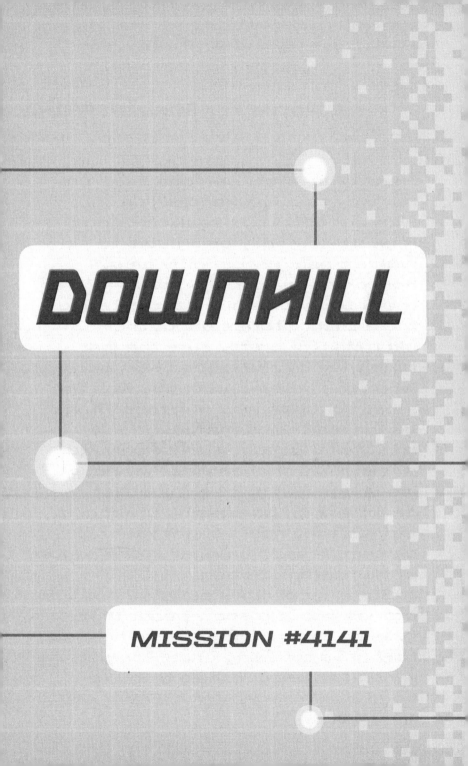

DOWNHILL

MISSION #4141

Here's the sitch: Ron and I are on our way to a weekend skiing trip with our class. I'm really looking forward to finally being able to ski without being chased by an evil henchman for once. Before I left for the trip, my parents started telling me ancient stories about their ski trips. I'm pretty sure the last time they hit the slopes was back when the horse and buggy was the most common way of travel. Thank goodness this is a student-only trip. Well, I guess student-only plus a few adult chaperones. Anyways, it's cringeworthy to think about the countless embarrassing childhood stories they could share with my classmates. I'd be right in the center of Humiliation Nation!

Some local news outlets have run stories about a snow beast that lives on the mountain we're headed to. I have a feeling once Ron gets wind of the scoop, he's going to head out in search of it. Either it's total urban legend, or it could be the work of a gene-splicing mad scientist. Let's hope it's just a myth.

Now I have to get back to Operation: Conceal Pandaroo. I mean, I couldn't leave home without my favorite Cuddle Buddy! How would I fall asleep without her? Hey, don't judge, those stuffed animals might definitely probably be worth something one day! Okay, I guess I can admit it's a little embarrassing. . . .

Name:	Amy Hall
Alias:	DNAmy
Wanted For:	Combining critters to make mutant real-life Cuddle Buddies
Strength:	Her brain
Weakness:	Stuffed animals
Last Seen:	Attending a Cuddle Buddy convention

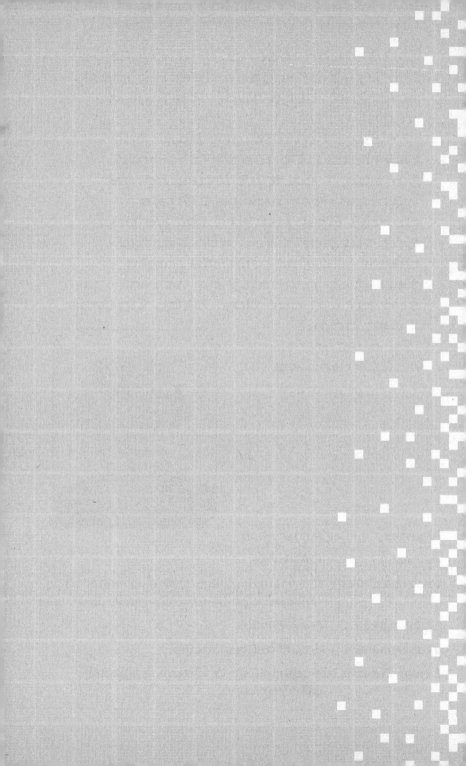

CHAPTER 1

SKI TRIP!

The biggest field trip of the school year was about to begin, and Kim Possible was psyched. She looked around the school parking lot. Everyone was wearing parkas and ski caps. Like her, they were totally ready to jump onto the yellow bus and head for the snow-covered slopes.

I'll really miss the drab hallways of Middleton High School, thought Kim. *Not!*

"Let's keep it moving, people!" Mr. Barkin, their teacher, bellowed. He was holding a clipboard and checking off names as students boarded the bus.

Kim's best friend, Ron Stoppable, joined the crowd of students. He was carrying two long skis over his shoulder.

"Stoppable!" Mr. Barkin said as he stepped in front of Ron. "Stow that gear!"

"Aye-aye, Mr. Barkin!" Ron said. He gave Mr. Barkin a cheerful salute. Then he spun toward the side of the bus and just missed whacking a kid in the head with his skis.

"Hey!" the kid shouted.

Ron spun again—to tell the kid, "My bad!" This time his skis nearly whacked *Kim* in the head!

"Ron!" Kim shouted.

Ron looked back sheepishly. "Sorry, KP," he said, finally tilting his skis upright and out of head-whacking range. "I am just totally psyched."

"Tell me about it," Kim said. "It's been so long since I've skied without some awful henchman after me."

For Kim, skiing away from henchmen was only one small part of saving the world on a regular basis. As a teenage global crime fighter, Kim often found herself dealing with wicked villains, evil plots, and lots of exploding things, too.

Suddenly, a nearly naked rodent popped out of Ron's pocket. It was Ron's beloved pet, Rufus. He was wearing a teeny little purple scarf and matching purple hat.

Rufus was excited, too. He punched his tiny front paws in the air.

Kim was no fan of hairless rodents. But for a mole rat, Rufus was pretty cool.

"Naked mole rat good to go," Ron said, patting Rufus's head.

Kim peeked inside her bag. Her favorite Cuddle Buddy, Pandaroo, was hidden inside. She just needed to make sure it stayed that way.

Just then, Ron and Kim caught sight of one of the kids waiting to board the bus. He was the only kid who looked ferociously miserable.

"Oh, look, Ron," Kim whispered.

"Alan Platt," Ron said with a knowing nod. "He deserves our pity, KP."

"So sad," Kim agreed.

"The biggest trip of the school year . . ."

"And his parents are the chaperones," Kim finished.

Ron looked grimly at the ground. "Humiliation Nation."

"Tragic," Kim said. She closed her eyes and observed a brief moment of silence. "But better him than me!" she finished brightly.

"Kimmy!" someone shouted.

"Mom?" Kim's mouth dropped open at the sight of her mother. She was wearing an old red parka that was so puffy, she looked like a parade float. And the matching hat actually had a pom-pom on it. For sure, a winter fashion *don't*.

"What's the sitch, Mom?" Kim asked, trying not to cringe. Her mother may have been a brilliant brain surgeon, but her fashion sense was limited to lab coats and hospital scrubs. "Did I leave something at home?"

"Not at all, honey," said Dr. Possible. "Your friend Bonnie called us." Dr. Possible glanced at Bonnie, who had just trotted over.

Bonnie and Kim had a long history. She was waving a little too cheerily at the moment. Kim narrowed her eyes suspiciously.

Calling Bonnie a friend was stretching it. The girl loved to cause trouble, especially for Kim. So a *happy* Bonnie was a *dangerous* thing.

"The Platts came down with the flu at the last minute," Dr. Possible continued.

Hearing this, Alan Platt grinned and high-fived the girl in line behind him. He was back in Normal Land.

Kim's dad walked over. He was a doctor, too—of

rocket science. To Kim's dad, being cool meant adjusting the room's temperature in Celsius. He was wearing a red parka just as old and ridiculously puffy as Kim's mom's. In other words, it was the "his" version of the winter fashion *don't*.

"So we grabbed our gear, dropped the boys at Nana's, and hightailed it right over," he told Kim.

Kim's eyes grew round as the reality of this nightmare dawned on her. "Wait," she said, hoping there might be some mistake. "You don't mean . . ."

"Meet our new ski-trip chaperones!" Bonnie announced as she whipped out her phone. "Smiles!"

Kim's dad pulled Kim between him and his wife as Bonnie took the picture. Everyone was grinning—except Kim.

A few minutes later, Kim's parents left to grab the rest of their gear, and Ron went to store his skis, leaving Kim alone with Bonnie.

"Wow," Bonnie said. "You know, it just occurred to me that some people might find it humiliating to have their parents along on a class outing." She dangled her phone in front of Kim's face and smiled evilly. "Especially someone with a big photo spread in the yearbook."

"You did this to me on purpose, Bonnie," Kim snapped.

"You are so paranoid," Bonnie huffed, rolling her eyes. "I think your parents are"—she glanced at Kim's father, who stood holding a strange case—"cute."

Kim frowned. The trip was supposed to be fun, but now she'd have to spend it doing parental damage control.

"Whatcha got there, Dr. P?" Ron asked, pointing to the strange case Kim's dad was holding.

"My homemade snowboard," Dr. Possible explained. As an expert in astrophysics, he was always inventing things. "I'm ready for shreddy!" Dr. Possible said, grinning at Ron.

Ron looked horrified at this parental use of teen lingo. "Excuse me?" Ron said.

"Dad's trying to act cool." Kim groaned and rolled her eyes in total embarrassment. "I'm doomed."

CHAPTER 2

"OOH!" Kim's mom said brightly, clapping her gloved hands. "I know a fun travel game that Kimmy used to love playing on family trips!"

"When she wasn't begging for a rest stop, that is," Kim's father added.

Everyone on the bus cracked up. Everyone but one person.

Kim sat toward the rear of the bus, glowering with her arms folded across her chest. The scenery was gorgeous—snow-covered trees and sky-high mountains—but Kim didn't care. She was too busy thinking of ways to disappear from this trip without anyone noticing.

Ron sat next to her reading the newspaper. "Incredible!" he said.

"I know," Kim agreed through clenched teeth. "Bonnie *will* pay for this."

"No, I mean *this*," Ron said, shoving the *Weekly Wonder* newspaper at her. "Check it out, KP. We're heading straight into the lair of the beast."

"'The Snow Beast of Mount Middleton Makes Tracks,'" Kim read aloud. She peered at the blurry photo below the headline. Rufus looked at it, too, whimpering in fear. Kim had to admit, it *could* have been a picture of the tracks of some strange animal. It also could have been an aerial photo of North Dakota. Or anything else in the world!

"Right," Kim told Ron. "From the same hard-hitting journalists who broke the Frog Boy story."

"I was personally touched by Frog Boy's struggle to fit into a world that could never truly accept him," Ron said seriously.

"Ron—" Kim said as she shoved the paper back at him. "*Look* at this picture. It could be *anything*."

"That's why the *Weekly Wonder* is offering five thousand dollars for a clear photo of the beast!" Ron cried.

Just then, Ron looked around. Everyone on the bus was staring at him.

"You don't really believe all that hooey, do you,

Stoppable?" Mr. Barkin asked from his seat behind Ron. He was wearing a parka with a portrait of his large cat, Lady Whiskerboots, on the back.

"Thank you, Mr. Barkin," Kim said to her cat-obsessed homeroom teacher. She frowned at Ron. "Some of us have *real* issues to deal with this weekend."

Ron lifted his eyebrows. "Like helping your parents with a sing-along?" he asked, pointing toward the front of the bus.

"Here we go!" chirped Kim's mom.

"Join in, Kimmy!" called her dad. He turned to the kids near him and dropped his voice to a whisper. "Did you know that Kim has a beautiful singing voice?" He put his arm around his wife, and they began to sing. *"Ninety-nine bottles of pop on the wall, ninety-nine bottles of pop . . ."*

Ron happily joined in. *"You take one down, pass it around . . . ninety-eight bottles of pop on the wall. Ninety-eight bottles of pop . . ."*

Soon everyone was singing. And Kim slid slowly down in her seat.

This was going to be the longest weekend of her life.

CHAPTER 3

"MAKE SURE YOU COLLECT ALL YOUR PERSONAL BELONGINGS!" Kim's dad called to the students on the bus. They had just pulled up to the ski lodge.

After leaving the bus, Ron strapped a huge pack onto his back.

"Ready to find that snow beast?" someone asked him in a low voice. He turned to see Mr. Barkin towering over him.

"Mr. B?" said Ron. "I don't get it. I thought you—"

Mr. Barkin clapped a meaty palm over Ron's mouth. "Stoppable, do you want the whole class going after the five Gs? Besides, I promised Lady Whiskerboots I would buy her a cat condo and the reward just about covers the initial deposit." Mr.

Barkin held up a crinkled magazine article featuring a luxurious cat condo. Ron had to admit, it was pretty nice.

"Oh . . . I gotcha," Ron said after Mr. Barkin removed his hand. Rufus got it, too. The mole rat rubbed his fingers together in the universal *show me the money* sign.

"What about Rufus?" Ron asked. Certainly his pet deserved a share.

"Tell you what, Stoppable—" Mr. Barkin said. "You help me get that photo, and I'll cut you in for two percent." He held up two fingers. "How you divvy it with your hairless pal is your business."

"Deal!" Ron said with a crafty smile, as though he'd just struck an incredible bargain. "Catch you later, KP!" he called to Kim.

"Ron? Where are you going?" There was desperation in Kim's voice. He *couldn't* leave her alone in Humiliation Nation!

"That reminds me of the cutest Kimmy story!" Kim's mom said—*loudly.* "So, we're on our first family ski trip," Dr. Possible was saying to Bonnie and a group of kids. "Kimmy's two years old and she takes off her clothes in the middle of the lodge. . . ."

Kim hadn't felt this much panic since the evil Dr.

Drakken threatened to melt her with magma!

Time to take control of the situation, Kim decided. Quickly, she pulled her mother aside. "Mom! Not now. Not ever," she cried.

"Oh, honey," said Dr. Possible. "Two-year-olds have been known to strut around stark naked." She laughed and looked over Kim's shoulder. "Am I right?"

"Absolutely," Bonnie agreed, smiling smugly at Kim. "Please, go on!" Bonnie said as she snapped another picture.

CHAPTER 4

"SHOULDN'T WE HAVE MULES OR SHERPAS OR SOMETHING?" Ron asked between heavy breaths as he trudged through the snow after Mr. Barkin. They had only been walking for twenty-three minutes, but to Ron, it seemed like weeks.

Rufus smirked from his place on the top of Ron's backpack. To Rufus, Ron *was* the Sherpa!

"When I snow-hike with Kim, we get Sherpas," Ron went on. Of course, Ron's snow adventures with Kim were usually in exotic places like Nepal. And she was the one who did most of the planning.

"You're not traveling with Sherpas today, son," Mr. Barkin snapped as he climbed to the top of a small hill. "Up here, you gotta earn your two percent. . . .

Wait a minute. . . ." Mr. Barkin stopped in his tracks. "You hear something?"

Ron glared at his teacher. "Teeth chattering? Knees knocking? Bladder sloshing? That's *me*!"

Barkin held his finger to his lips. "Shhh . . . Listen."

Just then, the snow-covered pine trees shook, and a roar thundered across the mountain.

"Snow beast!" Ron and Mr. Barkin shouted. Their prize photo—not to mention fame and fortune—was straight ahead!

Mr. Barkin started running. "For Lady Whiskerboots! Get a move on, Stoppable!" he called.

"It's on! It's on!" Ron cried, sprinting.

Mr. Barkin pointed. "Over there."

"Wait!" Ron noticed some trees moving off to their right. "It changed direction!"

He and Mr. Barkin lunged toward the moving trees. Just then, the snowy ground beneath their feet gave way, and they slid down a steep slope. Suddenly, the slope came to an end. "Whoa!" they screamed as they shot over the edge of a sheer cliff. Far below, a deep bank of snow broke their fall.

Ron sat up, shaking the snow out of his face.

Amazingly, he wasn't hurt—his landing had been pretty soft. "Rufus!" Ron cried, noticing a small mole rat–shaped hole in the snow beside him. "Rufus, you okay?"

Rufus sat up. He gave Ron a thumbs-up.

"Where's Mr. Barkin?" Ron asked.

The snow beneath Ron started to move. Then it picked him up and shoved him out of the way! Ron suddenly realized *why* he'd had such a soft landing. He'd fallen on top of Mr. Barkin!

Mr. Barkin grunted and shook himself. "It got away!" he cried.

Suddenly, there was another thunderous roar. Rufus whimpered and darted behind Ron.

"I-i-it's coming back!" Ron stammered as the trees in front of them parted. Then a shadowy creature stepped in front of them. Ron let out a terrified yell. Rufus clung to Ron's face in pure panic.

"Calm down, Stoppable!" Mr. Barkin said. "It's a human."

Ron blinked. He could see a woman approaching them, giving a little wave. "Thanks for noticing." She was a rather wide woman with glasses and a gap between her two front teeth. She had a bowl haircut and was dressed in drab shades of brown. A strange stuffed animal dangled from a piece of string around her neck. It looked like a tiny otter with wings.

"We thought you were the snow beast," Ron told the woman as he gently pulled Rufus off his face.

"Not that you look beastly in any way, ma'am," Mr. Barkin added quickly.

"Oh, puh-leeze!" the woman scoffed. "Don't tell me you believe that silly fairy tale."

"No-no-no," Mr. Barkin said, hiding the camera behind him.

"Oh, no," Ron agreed.

"I'm Amy Hall," the woman said. "Pleased to meet you, Mr. . . . ?"

"Barkin. Steve Barkin."

Amy stepped closer to Mr. Barkin and batted her eyelashes at him. "Say, Steeeevie—"

"I prefer Steve," Mr. Barkin said firmly.

"That makes two of us," Amy said coyly. "And who is this adorable creature?" she asked, noticing Lady Whiskerboots's portrait on Mr. Barkin's parka.

Mr. Barkin immediately softened. "That is an image of the most beautiful cat who ever existed," he said, wiping a tear from his eye.

"Aw, that is so cute! Anyhoo, I got all turned around up here. Would you mind leading me back to the lodge?"

"Actually, we—" Mr. Barkin began. But he didn't get to complete his thought.

"Would be tickled pink!" Ron finished.

Amy giggled and punched Mr. Barkin in the arm. "Pink is my favorite color!"

Mr. Barkin rubbed his arm. "Excuse us," he growled. He pulled Ron away. "What about the photos?"

"The photos can wait, Mr. B. Besides, maybe she can help us find the snow beast," Ron said, gesturing toward Amy.

"Stoppable—" Mr. Barkin began.

"Stevie," Amy called with a friendly wave, "the lodge awaits us."

"Just think of how happy Lady Whiskerboots will be soaking in rays on her cat condo rooftop," Ron continued.

"You have a point," Mr. Barkin admitted. Then he stomped over to Amy. "Ma'am," he said, "please follow me."

"To the ends of the earth, Stevie," Amy promised as she toddled after him.

They walked quickly to get out of the cold, none of them hearing the horrible roar that came from the trees behind them.

CHAPTER 5

"SO, YOU BUILT YOUR OWN SNOW-
BOARD, DR. POSSIBLE?" Bonnie asked as
she peered at Dr. Possible's strange case.

Kim's father grinned. "You'd be surprised at what
you can cobble together with odds and ends from
around the Space Center."

"I'd love to see it in action," Bonnie said. She
whipped out her phone. A picture of Dr. Possible's
monstrosity would be a great addition to her "humil-
iate Kim" yearbook spread. After this trip, she might
even have enough photos for an additional spread.

Seeing the phone, Kim snowboarded over.
"Whoa! Slow down there, Dad!" Kim said.

"Kimmy?" said Dr. Possible.

Kim hopped off her snowboard and pulled her

father aside. This was a code red situation. She had to handle it just right, or it could end in major embarrassment.

"Yours is so much cooler than everyone else's," Kim said carefully. "You don't want to bum out the other guys, do you?"

"Gosh," said Dr. Possible, "I don't want to bum anybody out. Not me."

"Good, Dad. Real good," said Kim as she handed her helmet to her dad.

Okay, she thought, *situation normalized.* Kim smiled at her dad, then stomped off to talk to Bonnie.

"Is everything okay, Kim?" Bonnie asked, her voice full of fake concern. "You seem kind of stressed."

Kim gritted her teeth. Suddenly, there was a shout from halfway up the slope.

"Kim!" Ron cried as he snowboarded toward them. He was waving his arms wildly, like he was out of control. At the last moment, he cut into the snow sharply to stop.

"Ahhh!" Bonnie shouted as a wave of snow whooshed over her. "You did that on purpose!" she told Ron.

Kim smiled. She knew Ron was an excellent snowboarder. Bonnie was right—he'd sprayed that snow on purpose. But Kim wasn't about to let Bonnie know that. "Now who's paranoid, Bonnie?" Kim said. "It was an accident."

Bonnie growled and stormed off.

Once she was gone, Ron stopped flailing. He stood up straight, grinning.

"I owe you one," Kim told him.

"Awww . . . it was nothing," said Ron with a shrug.

"Did you find your snow monster?" Kim asked.

Rufus poked his head out of Ron's pocket and shook it.

Ron petted his naked mole rat and leaned toward Kim. "How much do you know?"

Kim shook her head.

Just then, Mr. Barkin wandered by with the new president of his fan club—Amy.

"I'm gonna buy Y-O-U a mug of hot cocoa, Stevie," Amy said, holding his arm.

"That's really not necessary," Mr. Barkin said. "I need to get back to the slopes."

"With mini-marshmallows," Amy sang, ignoring his protests.

Just then, Kim noticed the weird stuffed animal hanging on a string around Amy's neck. "Hey," Kim said as Amy walked past, "an OtterFly."

"That's right!" Amy said eagerly. She took off her necklace and showed it to Kim. "You collect Cuddle Buddies?" she asked excitedly.

Kim was suddenly aware of three things. Number one: some kids from her class—including Bonnie—were building a snowman behind her. Number two: they were *hearing* this conversation. And number three: Cuddle Buddies were ferociously nerd-tacular. "Well," Kim hedged as she glanced over her shoulder, "I've seen them at the mall. No big."

"'*Seen* them'?" Kim's mom repeated as she walked over. She smiled and petted Amy's OtterFly. "Kimmy went *wild* for those little things."

Kim winced. She glanced at her classmates. Yep, they were listening. This was *so* not helping her coolness rating.

"I'm the past president of the Cuddle Buddy Collector's Club!" Amy cried, shaking Kim's hand and pulling her into a hug. "It's so nice to find a fellow Cuddler."

Suddenly, there was a flash of light. Kim looked over her shoulder in horror. Bonnie stood there with her phone. "You two must have *so* much in common," Bonnie said snidely.

Kim managed to escape from Amy's bearlike hug, but stopping Amy's mouth was another story. "You meet the nicest people at Cuddle functions, don't you?"

Kim shook her head. "Well, I've never—"

"So, Kimmy, who's your fave?" Amy went on. "Mine's OtterFly, *obviously*!"

Kim blushed and tapped her head as though she were thinking. How could she stop the humiliation? She didn't want everyone at school to think she was a huge Cuddle Buddy nerd. "Well, it was a long time ago—"

"What was that one you would never let me wash?" Kim's mom asked.

Kim froze. "I don't—"

"Pandaroo!" Dr. Possible said. "That's it. You still sleep with that little guy, don't you? So cute. Li'l Pandaroo."

Behind her, Kim heard Bonnie giggle evilly. Kim could imagine the photo in the yearbook already, with the caption "Kim Possible, who still sleeps with her fave Cuddle Buddy, Pandaroo."

Would the embarrassment never end?

CHAPTER 6

RON FOUND KIM AT THE LODGE CAFÉ, LEANING OVER THE OUTDOOR RAILING. "Kim?" he asked gently.

"Bonnie knows about Pandaroo," Kim said, gazing at the sky. "Hope is lost."

"That's harsh . . ." Ron said. "Do you mind calling Wade for me? It's sort of an emergency."

"Your concern touches me," she said as she tapped her Kimmunicator.

A hologram of Wade popped up. He was the tech genius who helped Kim and Ron on their adventures. "Wade? What's the snow beast sitch?" Ron asked.

"I've got no historical sightings," said Wade. "No reliable local legends . . . nothing."

"*This* is your emergency? Wait, is Wade in on this?" Kim asked.

Ron leaned toward Kim, using his hand to cover his mouth. "Only if he delivers," he whispered softly.

"What were you talking about?" Wade asked once Ron put his hand down.

"Not about the *Weekly Wonder* reward, if that's what you're thinking," Ron said.

"Barkin already has me down for ten percent," Wade said.

"*Ten?*" Ron cried. He was only getting two—and he had to split it with Rufus!

"*If* I deliver," Wade added.

"Fine," Ron snapped. "Just call me if you find anything." Wade's hologram vanished. "Kim, you want to come with me and Mr. Barkin to track the snow beast?" Ron asked.

"Don't you get it, Ron?" Kim cried. "This weekend is now strictly damage control. If I don't stay on top of my parents every minute, I'll never be able to show my face in school again! I'm in Humiliation Nation!"

Kim was so upset she didn't even notice her father. He had walked into the café and heard every word.

"Let's move, Stoppable," Mr. Barkin said as he

walked up to them, playing with his camera. "Before that Amy woman force-feeds me cocoa again."

Ron, Mr. Barkin, and Rufus trudged back up the ski slopes. Mr. Barkin held his camera, ready to snap a picture at any moment.

"I think we're getting close," Ron said when he spied a giant footprint in the snow. It was so large that his entire body easily fit inside it.

Mr. Barkin grinned and snapped photos of the footprint. Just then, the trees rustled. "Something moved over there," Mr. Barkin said.

"It didn't sound beast-sized," Ron said.

Suddenly, something scrambled out from behind some low tree branches.

"Oh, it's just a dog. Hey, pup," Mr. Barkin said. The animal hopped through the snow, which was almost up to its neck. It was wagging its tail. "What are you doing way out here?"

Mr. Barkin moved to pet the little pup on the head, and the dog reached out its paw—only there was no paw. The dog's front paws had been replaced with red lobsterlike claws!

"CHEESE 'N' CRACKERS!" Mr. Barkin shouted as the claws snapped at him.

"Now *that's* a mixed breed," Ron cried, staring at the half dog, half lobster.

The dog snapped its claws again, then scurried across the snow on its six short lobster legs. Remembering the *Weekly Wonder* paycheck, Mr. Barkin raised his camera. He ran after the strange creature, snapping photos.

Suddenly, there was a deafening roar. The mutant dog whimpered and ran off. Then something big burst through the trees. It looked like a cross between a bear, a rabbit, and a rhinoceros. And it was snarling and roaring at them!

Ron froze, paralyzed with fear. "Snow beast," he said in a tiny voice as the beast continued to roar.

"No!" cried someone behind them. Suddenly, the creature calmed down.

"You naughty, naughty beastie!" Amy cooed as she walked over to the creature. She was holding the lobster-dog in her arms, and two figures in ski masks and goggles stood behind her. "You shouldn't have run off like that," Amy scolded the beast. "You had Mommy all worried!"

The snow beast fell backward on its haunches and wailed.

"Amy!" Ron said, grinning. "In the nick of time! You tamed the beast! You saved me!" He gave her a huge hug.

"Why did it listen to her?" Mr. Barkin asked suspiciously as he walked over. "And why did she say 'Mommy'?" he added.

Hmmm, thought Ron. Mr. Barkin had a point.

"Oooh, you're a clever one, Stevie," Amy said. Then she turned to one of the masked figures. "Get the camera!" she commanded.

"She wants the reward!" Ron said in shock. Then the masked figure crushed the camera in his hand. The pieces formed a pile on the ground. "Or not," Ron said quietly.

As Mr. Barkin struggled with the masked figure, he yanked off the man's ski mask. Only it wasn't a man. He had the *body* of a man but the head of a chicken!

Behind him, the other masked figure pulled off his ski mask, revealing a pig's head. The creature squealed.

Mr. Barkin was still gaping at the chicken man when the pig man hit him over the head with a rock.

He was completely knocked out. Then the pig man slung Mr. Barkin over his shoulder.

"Take them to the lab," Amy sang as chicken man picked up Ron by his backpack.

"Let me go!" Ron shouted, dangling in the air. The chicken man was pretty strong, considering he was just oversized poultry.

They all followed Amy, who climbed onto the back of the snow beast and headed across the white landscape.

CHAPTER 7

BACK AT THE LODGE, KIM WAS ABOUT TO HIT THE SLOPES FOR A MOMENT OF RELAXATION UNTIL SHE NOTICED HER FATHER PUTTING THE FINAL TOUCHES ON A SNOWMAN. He stuck a carrot right in the center of the snowman's face just as two of Kim's classmates walked over. She was going to have to take a detour to do some damage control.

"Nice outfit, Dr. Possible," one of the girls said, eyeing his ridiculously puffy parka. "It's, like, retro chic."

"Groovy," Dr. Possible said sincerely.

The girls cracked up at the old-folks slang and walked off.

Suddenly, Kim's father heard a noise behind him. He turned and saw Kim with her hand over her eyes, shaking her head.

"I was just making small talk," Dr. Possible said defensively. "Forgive me if that's out-of-bounds."

Kim looked at him. She was surprised at his hurt tone. "What do you mean?"

"We better be going, dear," Kim's mom said as she walked up behind her husband. She put her hand on his arm and frowned at Kim. "We wouldn't want Kimmy to be in 'Humiliation Nation.'"

Kim's eyes widened. "You *heard* me?"

Her parents just turned and walked away.

Kim sighed and looked at the sky. "Smooth move, Kim," she told herself. She looked at her snowboard. Maybe some time on the slopes by herself would make her feel better.

"You can't just go gallivanting all over the mountain!" Amy scolded the snow beast once they were back at her laboratory. "Imagine what people must think."

Mr. Barkin and Ron were strapped against metal tables on the opposite side of the lab. Rufus was strapped to a smaller, Rufus-sized table next to them.

"What is this place?" Mr. Barkin asked as he looked around the enormous space. There were machines everywhere.

"Just my homey little genetics engineering lab," Amy explained brightly. "Let me show you my favorite part." She leaped over to a wall and twirled around. She hit a switch, and a bank of lights blinded Ron and Mr. Barkin.

"Sweet mother-of-pearl . . ." Barkin said, blinking. When his eyes adjusted to the bright lights, he saw Amy again. She was standing in front of row upon row of shelves leading up to the high ceiling. The shelves were completely covered with stuffed animals.

"Every Cuddle Buddy ever made," Amy said proudly, gesturing toward the collection behind her.

"That's a lot of plush, lady," Mr. Barkin said.

"I collected them all," Amy continued. Suddenly, her tone changed, and she balled her hands into fists. "But it wasn't enough—"

A timer dinged.

"Gingersnap cookies!" Amy sang happily as she walked toward the oven.

"Uh, question," Ron said, still strapped to his table.

"Yes?" Amy asked, pulling on a pair of oven mitts.

"What's up with the monsters?" Ron nodded toward the pig man, the chicken man, the lobster dog, and the bear-rabbit-rhino snow beast.

"I wanted more," Amy said as she pulled a tray of cookies out of the oven. "To go where no Cuddler has gone before." She grinned. "Life-sized living Cuddle Buddies!"

"That's quite a leap," Mr. Barkin said from his table.

"Not if you're one of the world's foremost bio-geneticists," Amy chirped. "They called me DNAmy." She walked over and held out her tray of cookies. "They said I was mad at Cuddle Con! Gingersnap?"

Mr. Barkin narrowed his eyes. "Lady, you are . . ."

"Special?" Amy guessed.

"YOU ARE SICK!" Mr. Barkin yelled. "And WRONG!"

Amy was so startled she dropped her cookies.

"You're just a meanie, Stevie," Amy said with a pout. Then an evil smile slowly spread across her face. "But I can fix that."

CHAPTER 8

KIM SNOWBOARDED ACROSS THE SLOPES. When she reached the highest peak, she looked out and saw some displaced snow in the distance with a black pile. She made her way over to the suspicious area and looked down. *What's Mr. Barkin's destroyed camera doing out here in the snow?* she wondered. Something didn't feel right. She reached for her Kimmunicator and tapped it.

"Wade," Kim said as his face appeared as a hologram in front of her, "I think we have a situation. I'm standing over Mr. Barkin's destroyed camera and there are signs of a struggle. Mr. Barkin was last seen with Amy. Can you try searching the Cuddle Buddy website? They profile all major Cuddlers—" Kim caught herself. "Er, collectors."

"How'd you know that?" Wade asked.

"I logged on a few times, okay?" Kim said defensively. "They're a good investment."

Wade's face was replaced by the Cuddle Buddy website. He clicked to an entry on Amy. "Good call, Kim," said Wade.

Kim scanned the information. "OtterFly is her favorite and . . ." Kim stared at the screen. "She's a biogeneticist?"

"That's not all," Wade went on. "She was kicked out of her university for splicing experiments. Her nickname was DNAmy."

"An out-of-control geneticist," Kim said. She clenched a fist. "I should've paid more attention to Ron's snow beast talk. We need to hurry. Wade, is there a satellite that can scan the mountain for artificial reinforcements?"

"Sure thing, KP," Wade said. "Hoping we might find signs of a hidden scientific lab?"

"If it's not asking too much," Kim replied.

"You're on a roll," Wade told her. "Artificial reinforcements in a large cavern to the north." The hologram showed a picture of the site.

"I'm there." Kim took off on her snowboard. She just hoped she wasn't too late.

Meanwhile, inside her cavern lab, DNAmy ordered her pig man and chicken man to wheel Rufus and Barkin over to a giant machine. It had two small globes—one on each side—and a large center globe with zipper-like notches down the center.

"Wait!" Ron wailed in protest. "Why punish Rufus? Barkin's the one you're mad at!"

"That's it, Stoppable!" Mr. Barkin growled. "You can kiss your two percent good-bye!"

"We could have been so cute together, Stevie," Amy said as she pulled a pair of green goggles over her eyes. "Well, now you'll find out what it's like to be genetically fused with a hairless rodent."

"Huh?" Barkin looked over at Rufus, who waved. Then he shouted at Amy, "You are twisted!"

The doors on each of the smaller globes opened. A green glow leaked from the machine as Mr. Barkin and Rufus were wheeled inside.

Mr. Barkin struggled against his straps as the door to his globe hissed closed. "Tell Lady Whiskerboots I'll always love her!" Mr. Barkin called out.

Inside the other globe, Rufus's eyes filled with tears, and he waved to Ron. Still strapped to his table, Ron waved back miserably, watching the second door close.

Amy's gloved hands flew across the keyboard. The machinery began to crackle with electricity. A strange green liquid bubbled through a long plastic tube leading to the machine that held Mr. Barkin and Rufus.

Just then, Kim crept into the lab and ducked behind an instrument panel.

Meow.

Kim turned and saw a cat peeking out at her. *What a cute kitty,* thought Kim. Suddenly, the cat slithered out of the shadows—on a *snake's* body! It reared and hissed, revealing fangs dripping with poison.

Uh-oh, thought Kim. *Not so cute after all!*

The cat-snake struck, wrapping Kim in its coils. Kim tried to fight, but its grip was too tight. She tripped and fell down the stairs, flying headlong into the wall of plush animals. The snake let go, and Kim grabbed the first two plush toys she saw.

Somersaulting forward, Kim came face to face with the mad scientist. "Let them go, DNAmy," Kim shouted, holding up the Cuddle Buddies, "or I'll—" Suddenly, Kim noticed what she had in her hand.

"Pandaroo!" she cried in a little-girl voice. "SUPER-STAR EDITION? They only made *twelve* of these!"

Oinking and squawking, the pig man and chicken man ran toward Kim. She hurled the Cuddle Buddies at them, and the two slid into the wall of plush toys. Half the huge collection tumbled down on them.

Kim ran toward the scientist, but the snow beast jumped to block Kim's path. Amy grinned as the giant rabbit-bear-rhino picked up Kim and hopped over to Amy.

"If you like Cuddle Buddies, Kimmy," Amy said, motioning toward the giant machine that held Mr. Barkin and Rufus, "just wait until you see my genetic zipper in action!"

Machines hummed and sparks flew as Amy threw the switch. Blinding light and smoke poured from the genetic zipper. Finally, the machine's doors opened. Out came a huge, muscle-bound mole rat with a bad attitude. It snarled and bared its front teeth.

"Rufus!" Ron cried. "You're a mutant!"

"Gross," Kim said.

"Naked mole man," Amy stated proudly as she pulled the ugly creature into a hug, "my greatest splicing success yet!"

Kim looked up at the rabbit-bear-rhino snow

beast craftily. It still had her in its firm grip. "Hey, Snowy," Kim said, gesturing toward Amy. "Looks like your mommy's got a new favorite." The snow beast growled. "She doesn't care about you," Kim continued. "You're just another collectible to her."

With a roar, the snow beast dropped Kim and bounded toward the naked mole man. They rolled over and over, fighting paw to paw. Kim didn't waste any time. She ran over to Ron.

"Stop it!" Amy shouted at her mutants. "Stop it this instant! There's room in my heart for all of you!"

The beast lunged at the naked mole man with its horn, but the mole man dodged the thrust and kicked the snow beast backward. The beast landed against the wall of collectibles, and more plush rained down. Snarling, the naked mole man leaped onto a nearby machine and tried to pull it apart. He'd gone berserk!

Quickly, Kim undid the straps that held Ron to the table. "Thanks, KP," Ron said. "We've got to get Rufus back."

"And Mr. Barkin!" Kim reminded him.

"Right," Ron agreed. "Him, too."

CHAPTER 9

AS THE NAKED MOLE MAN CONTINUED TO ATTACK THE MACHINERY, HE RIPPED OFF A GIANT VENT AND THRUST IT INTO ANOTHER MACHINE.

"No!" Amy cried. "These materials are unstable! If you don't stop, this whole place is gonna blow!"

Just then, the naked mole man picked up Ron.

"Mr. Barkin!" Kim cried. "No!"

But Ron wasn't afraid. "Rufus!" he said to the naked mole man. "I know you're in there, buddy. It's me!" Suddenly, the naked mole man's face softened and he lowered Ron to the ground. "That's my Rufus!" Ron said happily. But the naked mole man's change of heart didn't last. He began snarling at Ron again. Ron ran toward Amy to make sure she didn't have any more tricks up her sleeve.

Kim kicked the naked mole man backward, and he fell into the genetic zipper. The doors slid closed. Kim ran to Amy's panel and threw the switch—in reverse. She had no idea if it would work, but she had to try.

"Don't!" Amy cried while Ron held her back.

Energy hummed, and the machine turned red. Finally, the doors slid open. A small naked mole rat peeked out.

"Rufus!" Ron cried as he picked up his pet. "You're okay!" He looked more carefully at his dazed animal friend. He was no longer naked. He was wearing a tiny brown snowsuit. "You're wearing Mr. Barkin's clothes!"

"Then what's Mr. Barkin wearing?" Kim asked with a shudder.

"Stoppable!" Mr. Barkin shouted from the zipper. "I need pants!"

Kim and Ron couldn't find anything for Mr. Barkin to wear but Amy's old purple bathrobe covered in adorably posed rubber duckies. Mr. Barkin put it on just as part of the ceiling began to cave in.

"Let's evacuate, people!" Mr. Barkin shouted.

"Just once, I wish the bad guy's lair didn't have to blow up!" Kim griped.

"No!" Amy cried as she ran toward her Cuddle Buddy collection.

Kim grabbed her arm. "You have to leave!"

Amy shook her off. "Not without my Cuddle Buddies!" she shouted, trying to gather them all into her arms, but it was an impossible task.

Just as Kim, Mr. Barkin, Ron, and Rufus ran out of the cave, a deafening explosion let loose, throwing them over the edge of a steep cliff. Luckily, some pine trees broke their fall as Cuddle Buddies rained down from the sky.

"We made it!" Ron cried.

"Great," Kim said. She was glad she'd made it out of the lab alive—but there was something she still had to do. "Now I need to find my parents and apologize."

The earth began to shake. A low rumbling sound filled the air.

"You might not get the chance," Mr. Barkin said.

"Avalanche!" everyone cried.

They slid down the trees and ran through the snow, pursued by a tidal wave of white.

"We'll never outrun it!" Mr. Barkin said. "Who will

make sure Lady Whiskerboots eats her low-carb high-protein breakfast?" he asked frantically.

Kim and Ron glanced at each other. That was what Mr. Barkin was concerned about?

Just then, a figure in a puffy red parka appeared on the horizon. It was zooming toward them at an incredible speed. It was Kim's dad on his home-made snowboard!

"No way!" Kim shouted.

"Get ready! No time to stop!" Dr. Possible shouted as he scooped the foursome onto his snowboard. "Hang on! This could get 'gnarly'!"

Rocket jets burst into flame at the back of the board, and they ploughed down the mountain just ahead of the avalanche. As they neared a huge gap, Dr. Possible increased the power on the jets and launched across it. The avalanche tumbled after them, falling into the gap, while they landed safely on the other side.

The jet-powered snowboard plunged down a steep slope.

Kim's mother spotted them from the front of the ski lodge. "There they are!" she cried.

"Awesome ride, Dr. P!" Ron shouted as they picked up speed.

Mr. Barkin let out a loud yell as the snowboard shot off the end of a ski slope.

Mr. Barkin covered his eyes and Ron shouted, "Woo-hoo!" as they sailed through the open air. Finally, the group came to a stop, landing upright in front of the lodge. They all stood there a moment, then fell over backward into a heap in the snow.

Kim struggled to sit up. All the kids in her class were standing in front of the lodge, cheering. They had seen the whole wild ride!

Kim smiled at her father. Then she reached up and wrapped her arms around his neck. He returned her hug, and she knew she had been forgiven.

Funny, thought Kim, *for the first time this weekend, I actually wish Bonnie were here to take our picture.*

"Dad," said Kim, "you're amazing."

Dr. Possible grinned at his daughter. "Oh, no big," he said.

CHAPTER 10

A FEW MINUTES LATER, TWO UNIFORMED POLICE OFFICERS ESCORTED DNAMY TO A POLICE CAR. "Come see me, Stevie!" she shouted over her shoulder to Mr. Barkin.

Mr. Barkin cringed.

Amy kissed the glass on the inside of the police car as it pulled away.

Kim looked at her mother, who was still gaping at the strange scene. "Mom, I am so sorry," Kim said.

Kim's mom put her arm around her daughter's shoulders. "Don't worry, honey," she said warmly. "Your father and I were teenagers once. Sometimes we forget what it's like." Then she gave her daughter a warm hug.

Click! A flash went off. "Isn't this a sweet moment . . ." Bonnie said snidely.

Kim's mom frowned. But it didn't bother Kim in the least.

Just then, a tall lanky woman with frizzy hair walked out of the lodge. "Bonnie!" she sang.

Bonnie whirled around to face the woman. "Mom?" she cried.

"Pumpkin!" Bonnie's mom chirped happily. She was wearing wide-rimmed glasses with purple frames, purple mittens, purple dangly earrings, and a purple ski sweater. She also had on plaid pants and pink leg warmers.

This was more than a fashion *don't*. It was a fashion *don't even think about it!*

Bonnie's mom pranced over and gave her daughter a tight hug.

Bonnie ducked out of her mom's embrace. "Mother, what are you doing here?" she demanded.

Bonnie's mom pinched her daughter's cheek. "I heard that you kids needed more chaperones, so I rushed right up."

"But . . . you can't!" Bonnie insisted.

"Now, Bon Bon," Bonnie's mom said, "don't go flying off the handle."

"Bon Bon?" Ron repeated.

"If everything isn't just so, little Bon Bon goes straight to pieces," Bonnie's mom said with a laugh.

"But why?" Bonnie squealed, clearly dying of embarrassment. "Who called you?"

"There're too many kids for just us to handle," said Kim's mother. "And I figured if Kimmy got to enjoy having *her* parents around, why not you, too, Bonnie?" Then Dr. Possible gave Bonnie a sly time-to-take-what-you-dished-out wink.

"This is going to be such fun," Bonnie's mom chimed in as she led her daughter away. "You have to introduce me to every single one of your little class-mates. I have so many Bonnie stories to tell them!"

Bonnie closed her eyes and sighed.

Kim couldn't believe it, but she was actually sorry the ski trip was almost over. *Oh, well,* thought Kim as she watched Bonnie's mother dragging her daughter away. There would always be Bonnie's yearbook spread to bring back the memories!

Kim smiled up at her own mother. "You rock, Mom," she said.

"You rock, too, Kimmy," said Dr. Possible. Then she wrapped her daughter in the warmest hug ever.

THE SNOW BEAST OF MOUNT MIDDLETON MAKES TRACKS

Recently, local mountain residents have reported sightings of a mysterious creature. Some describe it as a bear, others a rhinoceros. One man even claimed to have seen a gigantic rabbit. Despite these conflicting reports, all residents who have seen the creature agree it would strike fear into the heart of any brave explorer.

Many other residents have reported hearing a thunderous roar echoing across the mountain. The noise has been described as sickening and horrible, and one man claimed the feeling he got after hearing the roar was "definitely the opposite of cuddling with a Cuddle Buddy."

Currently, the only photographic evidence of the beast is a footprint that vaguely resembles the shape of North Dakota. Upon reviewing the photograph, local ski lodge owner Al Pine said, "Have you seen the picture? It could be anything!" Well, one thing is for sure: it is definitely something.

If you have any information about beast sightings, please contact the *Weekly Wonder* editorial staff. To avoid any confusion, yes, this is the same staff of hard-hitting journalists who broke the Frog Boy story. And no, the staff will not be addressing any additional Frog Boy–related inquiries at this time.

The *Weekly Wonder* is offering a $5,000 reward for a clear photo of the beast. If you do search for the beast, please note that the Sherpa union has gone on strike. Sherpas will not be available for the foreseeable future.

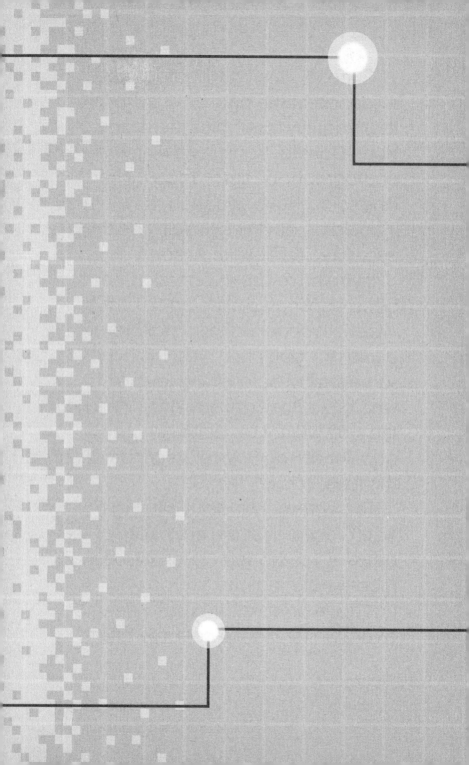

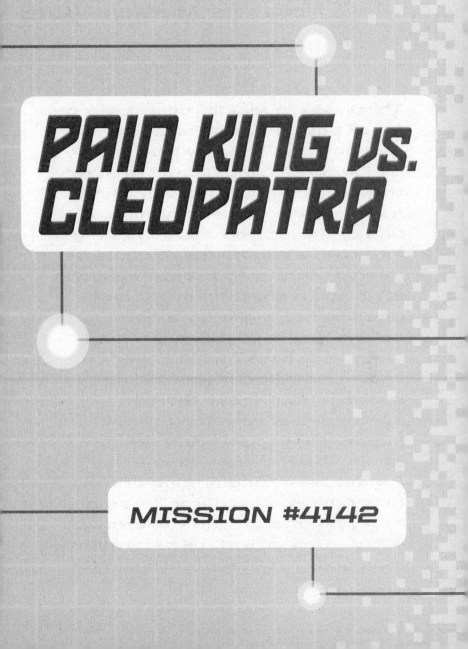

PAIN KING VS. CLEOPATRA

MISSION #4142

Notes for Mission #4142

This week in Middleton, there's a lot of action. First, there's a new Cleopatra's Closet exhibit at the Middleton Art Museum. I'm sure they've got extra security, but I hope no one steals anything. If one of her powerful talismans got into the wrong hands, it could be a major threat to the world. Wade is going to check in every now and then to make sure nothing suspicious is going on.

And not that I would ever know this without Ron telling me—repeatedly—but there's some sort of wrestling event happening in town. Something about Toe Pain and King Steal? I must be mixing up one of the two. Anyways, apparently it's a really big match and will draw an extra-large crowd full of wrestling maniacs . . . I mean, enthusiasts.

Ron and I are headed to the Middleton Mall now. He wants to check out the event opening for the latest wrestling something or other. I'm headed straight to Club Banana. I heard Club Banana just got in next season's line and some of it is inspired by Cleopatra herself! As a charter member of the Club Banana Club, I get early access to the launch. I can't wait to try it all on! That Cleopatra was one fierce lady, so I'm sure the fashion line will be a must-have.

Name:	Jackie Oaks
Wanted For:	Trying to gain powers so he can compete in wrestling matches
Strength:	His powers, when he is able to secure any
Weakness:	His power lies only in the object giving it to him
Last Seen:	At the Chicago GWA (Global Wrestling Association) match

CHAPTER 1

KIM POSSIBLE RACED DOWN THE DARK STREET. An angry mob was at her heels. "Pain! Pain! Pain! Pain!" the young men chanted.

"They're getting closer, KP!" cried Kim's best friend, Ron Stoppable.

Yeah, thought Kim, *tell me something I don't know!* "This way!" she called. Ron nodded and followed her down a narrow alley.

Garbage cans and trash were everywhere. Kim wrinkled her nose as she ran. So *not a good smell,* she thought. But maybe now they'd beat that annoying mob.

As they ran, Ron looked back over his shoulder. Ron's pet, Rufus, his head sticking out of Ron's pocket, looked worried. The naked mole rat was always nervous when Ron ran *one* way while looking *another.*

Just then, Rufus spotted a cluster of garbage cans right in front of them. He let out a concerned squeal, trying to warn Ron. Too late! *Crash!* Ron hit the cans and sent them scattering.

"Ron, over here!" Kim called from the shadows. He crouched beside her, next to a parked car. "I think we lost them," Kim whispered.

Ron exhaled, finally able to relax. Suddenly, a ferocious-looking dog reared up inside the car. *Ruff! Ruff! Ruff!*

"Ahhh! Teeth and slobber!" shrieked Ron.

Kim and Ron took off but didn't get far before bright headlights shined into their eyes. A red car raced out of the darkness and screeched to a halt in front of them. Three big guys hopped out, chanting, "Steel! Steel! Steel! Steel!"

Another *mob?* Kim thought. *Tough sitch!* "Come on!" she cried, and they raced the other way. When they reached a large metal door, Ron sighed with relief. This was it—finally! They'd reached the back entrance of their destination.

Ron tried the door, but it was locked. He glanced at his watch. Time was almost up. They *had* to get inside!

The building's front entrance wasn't an option. More chanting mobs of young people had completely swamped it.

"We'll never make it!" Ron groaned.

But Kim refused to give up. "There's gotta be another way in," she declared.

"Pain! Pain! Pain! Pain!" the first mob chanted as they tramped down one end of the alley toward Kim and Ron.

"Steel! Steel! Steel! Steel!" shouted the second mob as they marched toward them from the other end.

The yells soon merged into a single chant. "Pain! Steel! Pain! Steel! Pain! Steel!"

The two mobs were both headed toward the back entrance—and Kim, Ron, and Rufus were stuck in the middle!

So *not the place to be,* Kim thought. Reaching into her pack, she drew out her portable hair dryer, which also doubled as a grappling hook.

Kim pointed the device upward and pulled the

trigger. The hook shot into the air, dragging a long length of rope behind it. *Clink!* It attached itself to the roof of the building above.

Kim grabbed Ron with one arm and clutched the grappling device with the other. "Going up," she said as the rope retracted, lifting them to the roof.

Below them, the two mobs had surrounded the entire building. Trying to gain entrance, they pounded on the doors.

"Pain! Steel! Pain! Steel! Pain! Steel!" they chanted.

"C'mon, Kim, we've gotta get inside!" Ron said as they landed on the roof. But as he turned, Ron tripped and tumbled off the ledge!

CHAPTER 2

STILL CLUTCHING THE GRAPPLING DEVICE, KIM DOVE OVER THE EDGE OF THE BUILDING.

"Yahhh!" shrieked Ron as he fell. Rufus covered his eyes with his paws. He couldn't look!

But before they hit the ground, Kim reached out with her free hand and grabbed Ron. A split second later the device's rope stopped their fall.

But Kim, Ron, and Rufus were swinging toward a brick wall. Ron thought they'd be smashed to bits. At the last second, Kim kicked her legs out and they smashed through the building's air vent.

They tumbled down a long air shaft, burst through another vent, and landed inside the large building. After sliding across the shiny clean floor, they came to a stop against a decorative water fountain.

Hundreds of people were strolling calmly around the fountain. Not one of them had noticed Kim and Ron's dramatic entrance. In fact, all the people looked dazed and distracted.

Was this a secret lab filled with zombie-creating experiments? *No.* Was it an alien invasion of zoned-out pod people? *No way.* It was the Middleton Mall. And Kim was totally used to seeing people there marching around in a shopping trance.

No big, she thought. Jumping to her feet, she brushed herself off. "Next time we come to the mall, let's stick to the main entrance, okay?" she told Ron.

But Ron was barely listening. He was too busy grinning at a colorful banner that read WELCOME TO MIDDLETON MALL'S WRESTLING WRIOT. Outside, mobs of wrestling fans were still trying to push their way through the choked entrances. With Kim's help, Ron had already beaten the crowd inside!

Of course, Kim was a little annoyed that she'd had to surf an air shaft to do it. She glanced down at the dirty adventure gear she was wearing. "You know, I usually like to go home and change after a mission," she complained to Ron as she brushed some of the dirt from her clothes.

"No time for that, KP," he said.

"Okay. *Why?*" Kim asked.

Ron pointed to the center of the mall, at a giant stage surrounded by cheering fans.

"Steel! Pain! Steel! Pain! Steel! Pain!" chanted the audience of young people.

"The first hundred fans not to be trampled get a free GWA tour T-shirt!" Ron exclaimed.

"GWA?" said Kim. Then she spied the GLOBAL WRESTLING ASSOCIATION banner over the stage. Another sign behind the podium read WRESTLING WRIOT.

"How can you *not* know the Global Wrestling Association?" asked Ron. "It's only the most excellent sporting organization in the world."

Kim rolled her eyes while Ron joined in the cheering. "Steel Toe rules! Yeah!" he yelled.

"Pain! Pain! Pain!" a bunch of fans chanted right back.

Kim shook her head. "All this just because some wrestlers are making a mall appearance?" she said.

"Not just *some*," Ron pointed out. "Pain King and Steel Toe."

Kim really didn't want to hear any more. But she *so* knew she would.

"Pain King's got a bionic eye," Ron went on. "Don't even think about looking into it, or you'll writhe on the floor in total pain!"

"And I suppose Steel Toe actually has steel toes?" Kim asked.

"Nah, that's just a publicity gimmick," Ron replied. "They're more like titanium, actually. A freak industrial accident."

Rufus let out an enthusiastic squeak.

Kim crossed her arms and shook her head. "Right," she said doubtfully.

Just then, an amplified voice boomed through the mall. "Listen up, Middleton! Are you ready for action?"

Wild cheers rose from the packed crowd. Kim turned to see a very short man in a silk suit standing behind the podium.

"Are you ready for head-bumping, chest-thumping, back-breaking, ground-shaking con-fron-ta-tion?!?" yelled the short man.

"Yeah, baby!" the crowd shouted back.

Kim jerked her thumb toward the man onstage. "Is that Pain Guy?" she asked.

"No way!" Ron said. "That's Jackie Oaks, founder of the GWA."

"Now, here's a little secret," said Jackie Oaks in a loud voice. "These two world-class athletes that I'm about to bring out hate each other's guts!"

Cheers and wild applause broke out as Pain King entered. He was massively muscled and wore a blue wrestling suit and mask, topped by a golden crown.

"Pain! Pain! Pain! Pain!" chanted Pain King's fans.

From the other side of the stage came Steel Toe, his titanium foot clanging with every step. Steel Toe sported green trunks and even more muscles than Pain King.

"Steel! Steel! Steel! Steel!" chanted Steel Toe's admirers. The cheers and shouts continued until they merged into a single chant. "Steel! Pain! Steel! Pain! Steel! Pain! Steel! Pain!"

The two wrestlers met in the center of the stage. Steel Toe flexed his muscles while Pain King waved to the crowd. Then they immediately began pushing and shoving each other.

"Okay, I'm in the mall, and I'm *not* shopping," Kim griped. "What's wrong with *this* picture?"

CHAPTER 3

KIM HAD SEEN ENOUGH OF THE WRESTLING STAGE SHOW. She was about to leave when Ron stopped her.

"Wait, wait, wait!" he insisted. "Wrestling is more than two guys taking each other down. It's also a war of words."

Ron pointed to the stage as Steel Toe and Pain King flexed their pecs and glared at each other.

"You're going *down*!" Pain King declared.

"No, *you're* going down!" bellowed Steel Toe.

"No, *you're* going down!" barked Pain King.

"No, *you're* going down!" Steel Toe shot back even louder.

Kim rolled her eyes. "Yeah," she said, "they're poets. Look," she told Ron. "Club Banana's doing a tie-in with the museum's Cleopatra's Closet exhibit. That's where I'll be."

Kim snaked her way through the mob and headed for her favorite boutique. Outside Club Banana, Kim smiled at the colorful signs advertising the boutique's new line of ancient-Egyptian-inspired styles.

After pushing through the boutique's doors, she took a deep breath of Club Banana air—the crisp scent of new clothes and price tags. She raced for a table full of trendy cargo pants, pressed her cheek against the perfectly folded pile, and sighed. "Hello, civilization," she said.

"Oh, my gosh," cried a cool-looking salesperson wearing a teal shirt with matching earrings. "How much do you love Cleo's Cargos?" she asked Kim as she approached.

"Way much," Kim replied. She smiled at the girl, who was already wearing a pair of the hot new cargos.

Kim began flipping through the pile of pants looking for the perfect pair. The salesperson whipped out a green pair from the bottom of another stack.

"You'd look good in Giza green," Kim and the salesperson said at the very same time.

"Jinx!" they both cried, turning and pointing at each other.

Kim laughed. "You owe me a soda!" she told her new friend.

Meanwhile, outside Club Banana, the atmosphere was far less friendly. In the courtyard of the Middleton Mall, the Wrestling Wriot was getting even more riotous.

"It makes me sick to look at you, lead foot," bellowed the chest-thumping Pain King.

"You will be so much sicker when I stomp you with cold hard steel!" yelled Steel Toe.

Suddenly, Pain King lunged at Steel Toe, and the two began to fight. The crowd went wild!

"Let's go!" Pain King cried. "Right here! Right now!"

As the two massive wrestlers grappled center stage, Jackie Oaks jumped between them. The two athletes towered over the short promoter.

"Now, now, boys," Jackie said, trying to separate the wrestlers. "Save it for Mayhem in Middleton." Then he winked and added, "Good seats still available, folks!"

But the two wrestlers would not quit. Finally, Pain King shoved Steel Toe so hard he nearly fell.

"You're going down!" roared Pain King.

Steel Toe charged his opponent, slamming his head into Pain King's belly. Pain King howled in, well, *pain*.

Suddenly, the chaos onstage spread to the fans. Admirers of Steel Toe started butting heads with fans from Pain King's camp. Then they started wrestling in the aisles!

Ron Stoppable tried to escape. But as he pushed through the crowd, a Pain King fan grabbed him and forced him into a headlock.

"Awwww!" squawked Ron. Then the crazed fan grabbed Ron's ankles and swung him around in a wide circle.

Inside Club Banana, Kim was oblivious to the chaos. She was too busy at the checkout counter, buying her new Cleo's Cargos.

"Do you belong to our Club Banana Club?" the salesperson asked.

"Charter member," Kim replied, handing over her club card.

The salesperson looked at the card and did a double take. "Kim Possible?" she cried in a high-pitched voice. "I thought it was you. The stuff you do is so amazing."

Kim blushed. "Ah, it's no big, but thanks."

"I'm Monique," the salesperson replied, shaking Kim's hand. "Just moved here."

"Cool," said Kim. "Where do you go to school?"

"Middleton High," said Monique.

Kim grinned. "Me too!"

"I start Monday," Monique said.

A new best friend, for sure! "You totally have to let me show you around," Kim insisted. "And you should definitely join the Martial Arts Club! I'm one of the co-captains."

"Deal!" said Monique as they shook hands again.

Suddenly, Ron Stoppable's terrified scream echoed through Club Banana from outside the store. "Kim!" he howled.

Kim glanced outside and saw Ron being tossed around among the crowd. She grabbed her stuff and bolted. "See you at school!" she called to Monique. Then she raced through the mall to—*once again*—rescue Ron.

CHAPTER 4

WHAT IS THIS? Kim thought as she entered the mall's courtyard.

Wrestling insanity had broken out both onstage and off. Young people were flailing all over the place, imitating their favorite wrestlers' moves. Above the shouts and flying bodies, Kim could hear Ron's screams.

"Scuse me! Pardon me!" Kim cried as she leaped over a tangle of guys tussling on the ground.

As Kim hurried through the crowd, two women rose up to block her path. Without even slowing down, Kim leaped onto their shoulders. The women tried to grab her, but she gracefully slipped out of reach. Then she flipped to the center of the mob, grabbed Ron, and launched herself smoothly onto the stage.

Kim's actions were so graceful and amazing that everyone stopped fighting for a moment just to stare up at her.

Even promoter Jackie Oaks was impressed. He pushed Steel Toe and Pain King aside. Then he rushed across the stage to corner Kim.

"Oh, honey, that was some performance," Jackie Oaks gushed. "You ever think about a career in professional wrestling?"

"*So* not," Kim replied.

Jackie Oaks frowned. He reached into his suit and drew out two tickets, which he thrust into Kim's hand. "I'll tell you what," he said. "Here's two passes to Mayhem in Middleton. Enjoy yourself on Jackie." Then he showed them the offstage exit.

Ron stared in awe at the tickets. "These are backstage passes!" he cried. "You get to go *backstage* with backstage passes! Where the *backstage* is!"

"And hang out with some guy named Steel Cage?" Kim asked in a *so*-not-interested tone.

"Uh, KP, Steel *Toe* is a guy," Ron explained, trying to be patient. "Steel *Cage* is, well . . . a cage."

"You take 'em," Kim said, handing over the tickets.

"You can't just give them away!" Ron cried. "Do you know what these are worth?"

Then Ron looked down at the tickets in his hand and stopped short in his tracks.

"Okay," he said, "you *can* give 'em to me."

But Kim had kept walking. She was already ten paces ahead.

"Hey," Ron said, catching up. "Let's go back to your house and watch wrestling so we can get psyched to watch . . . *wrestling*!"

Kim shook her head. "Not tonight. I'm going to the Cleopatra's Closet exhibit at the Middleton Art Museum. It's a special preview for Club Banana frequent buyers."

Ron could not believe what he was hearing. "You'd rather see some dead queen's clothes than watch *Steel Toe's Night of a Hundred Bruises* with me?" he cried.

Kim sighed. "My answer would have to be— *Hello? Yeah! See ya!*"

Kim walked away, leaving Ron alone with his tickets.

"Cleopatra," scoffed Ron. "Like anybody's going to remember *her* ten years from now!"

Later that night, Kim arrived at the Middleton Art Museum. Over the huge entranceway, a banner proclaimed: SEE THE CONTENTS OF CLEOPATRA'S CLOSET.

Since the exhibit was open only to Club Banana frequent buyers, only a dozen other lucky folks were in attendance. Kim smiled when she spotted her brand-new friend. They were both wearing the same Giza green Club Banana cargo pants.

"Monique!" Kim cried. "I should've known you'd be here."

"Exclusive preview? The queen's accessories? Girl, it is all good," Monique replied.

The girls paused to admire each other's Cleo-wear. "I love your pants!" Monique exclaimed with a wink.

"And you? Very Cleo," Kim said approvingly.

Moments later, a tall woman wearing a purple dress greeted the crowd in front of a giant door.

"It's my pleasure to welcome you to this special Club Banana preview of Cleopatra's Closet," the woman announced. But when she threw open the door to start the tour, she cried, "Oh, my goodness!"

The lights in the exhibit were off. On the floor lay a museum security guard, tied up with a gag over his mouth. From the darkness beyond the door came the sound of breaking glass.

A burglar was looting Cleopatra's Closet!

CHAPTER 5

KIM QUICKLY PUSHED THE REST OF THE CROWD BACK. "Call security and stay together!" she cried.

Then Kim reached for her Kimmunicator around her neck. She touched it once.

"Wade!" she called. "Trouble at the Middleton Museum. Can you tap the security cam?"

"Tapping," Wade replied. Wade was the computer genius who often helped Kim and Ron save the world!

Then Kim heard another crash in the exhibit room. There was no time to wait for Wade! Kim raced through the gloomy museum until she noticed a small dark figure enter a stairwell at the back.

Kim tailed the burglar up the stairs and onto the

museum's roof. But by the time she got there, the burglar had vanished.

Suddenly, a brilliant flash nearly blinded her. It came from behind a big air-conditioning unit.

"You are *so* busted!" Kim declared as she charged forward. There was another flash of light, and she heard a doglike bark. A shadowy figure jumped out from behind the air conditioner and ran across the roof.

Whoa, thought Kim, *what* is *that thing?* From the neck down, it looked like a normal man, but instead of a human head, the fleeing figure had big ears and a doglike snout. And he was glowing!

Guess that explains the bark, thought Kim, taking off. She chased the figure to the edge of the roof.

Got you now! Kim thought—until the burglar leaped right off, sailing an impossible distance. The burglar easily landed on another roof across a wide, busy street.

Nobody in the world could have made that jump—nobody *human,* that is.

Across town, Kim's twin brothers, Tim and Jim Possible, were sitting in their living room with Ron

Stoppable and Rufus. They all were watching GWA's *Chaos in Chicago* on a big-screen TV.

"Woo-hoo! Toes of steel!" yelled Ron.

"Oooh! Pain King's down!" cried Tim.

"Duh, Pain King never beats Steel Toe," declared Jim.

Suddenly, Kim burst into the room. "Ron!" she cried. "You won't believe what happened tonight."

"Shhh!" hissed Tim, Jim, and Ron, their eyes glued to the screen.

"Come on now, man!" bellowed Pain King. "Let's see what you got!"

"You're going down!" Steel Toe replied.

Kim rolled her eyes as she waited for a commercial break.

Beep-beep! Beep-beep! Kim's Kimmunicator chirped and she tapped it. A hologram of Wade appeared before her. "What's the sitch, Wade?" she asked.

"Shhh!" Ron, Jim, and Tim hissed again.

"Sorry, Wade," Kim whispered, stepping away from the TV. "Go ahead."

"The only thing stolen from the museum was a small talisman," Wade informed her. "It was a gift to

Cleopatra from the high priest of Anubis, the jackal-headed Egyptian deity of mummification."

On the hologram in front of her, Wade showed Kim the golden half-moon-shaped amulet. It hung on a golden chain.

"A mummy?" said Kim. "Gross. I bet she would've rather had nice earrings."

"Don't be too sure," said Wade. "This talisman was supposedly enchanted."

"Oh, come on," Kim scoffed. "Who would believe that?"

"Maybe that glowing guy on the roof?" Wade suggested.

"Good point," said Kim. "What's it supposed to do?"

"Superhuman strength," Wade said ominously.

"Great," Kim said with a sigh. "Well, at least it's not immortality, I guess. Thanks, Wade."

When *Chaos in Chicago* broke for a commercial, Ron finally walked over to Kim.

"So, how were the queen's clothes?" he asked.

"I barely got to see them," Kim replied. "Right after I met up with Monique, the museum was robbed by some glowing animal-headed guy!"

"That's nice," said Ron as if he wasn't paying attention. Then the words sunk in and Ron blinked in surprise.

"Wait a minute!" cried Ron. "Who's *Monique*?"

CHAPTER 6

KIM WAS PUZZLED. Ron seemed more interested in Monique than he was in a robber with a dog's head!

"Monique's a new friend," Kim said. "Really great. Anyway, the thief stole an ancient enchanted talisman!"

"Whoa, whoa, whoa! Back up," insisted Ron. "How can I not know about a new friend?"

"I met her at Club Banana," Kim explained. "Then again at the museum . . . before I *chased the glowing robber.*"

"So, what's she like?" asked Ron.

"The robber?" said Kim.

"The *friend*, Kim," Ron replied. "The '*new* friend.'" He made air quotes with his fingers.

"Focus!" Kim insisted. "There's a glowing guy running around Middleton with some kind of supernatural powers."

"Okay, okay," said Ron. "Why don't we hit Bueno Nacho and you can fill me in?"

"No, thanks," Kim replied. "Monique and I stopped for smoothies on the way home."

Ron blinked in shock. "Smoothies?"

An hour later, Ron was sitting in a booth at Bueno Nacho. His only company was Rufus. Both of them missed Kim.

"I can't wait to tear into this naco, but I'm not feeling so hungry. I'm worried, Rufus. Since when does Kim drink smoothies?" he asked.

Rufus jumped into a plate of grande nacho chips. He let out a squeal of support for Ron, then drowned his sorrows in cheesy nachos. He missed Kim, too.

"I'm seeing a pattern here, Rufus," Ron said. "Kim does her thing, I do my thing, and pretty soon, we're doing *different* things. Plus, she's doing those different things with Monique."

Rufus swallowed his bite of nachos and looked

at his friend. Just because Ron wasn't hungry didn't mean he had to wait. Besides, more nachos for him!

"Maybe I'm just blowing this whole Monique thing out of proportion," Ron continued. "I know it's okay to make new friends, but this is *Kim* we're talking about. I just don't want anything to ever come between us."

Rufus glanced up from the plate of cheesy nachos. He wiped cheese off his chin with his paws. He picked up an extra-cheesy nacho chip and held it out to Ron.

"Thanks, Rufus," said Ron a little sadly. Then he brightened up. "Hey, maybe I should give Monique a chance. If Kim likes her as much as she says she does, then I'm sure I would, too! Kim does have excellent taste in friends if I do say so myself." He let out a breath and smiled.

Ron felt better already. "I'll bet tomorrow everything's back to normal," he assured himself.

But the next morning, when Ron dropped by Kim's house, he discovered things weren't back to normal. Not even close.

"Good morning, Dr. Possible," he said when

Kim's mom answered the door. "Is Kim ready for school yet?"

"Actually, you just missed her, Ron," Kim's mom replied. "I think she said something about meeting her new friend, Monique."

Ron's face fell. "Monique?" he choked out. Rufus shook his head sadly.

"Oh!" exclaimed Kim's mom. "And I'm going to be late for my cranial bypass. Say hi to your folks."

Kim's mom grabbed her bag and dashed off, leaving Ron standing on the front porch.

But Ron didn't stay there for long. He thought of the plan he came up with at Bueno Nacho. To save a friend, he'd make a friend. *Yeah,* he thought, *time to fight a new friendship with . . . a new friendship.*

At lunch that day, Ron put his friendship plan into action. When he saw Kim and Monique chatting in the school cafeteria, he walked over to join them.

"And then once, I was saving this desert prince from some terrifying squad, and the back of my skirt was totally covered in beetles. *The whole time!*" Kim was telling Monique between bites of fruit cup.

"No way!" Monique cried as she ate her yogurt.

"I could have died," said Kim, waving her spoon. "He almost did!"

Suddenly, a bag of warm doughnuts dropped on the table in front of Kim. She looked up—into the smiling face of Ron Stoppable.

"Hello, ladies," Ron said smoothly.

"Ron! What are you doing here?" asked Kim.

"Well," said Ron as he sank into an empty chair, "can't I dine with my best friend? And her new friend . . ."

Ron stared pointedly at Monique, and Kim made the introductions. "Uh, Ron . . . Monique. And vice versa," she said awkwardly.

Ron reached into the bag and made a pastry offering to Monique. "Bear claw?" he asked.

"No, thanks," Monique replied. "I'm a vegetarian."

Ron stared at the pastry.

"Uh," he said, "I'm pretty sure it's *imitation* bear."

"She's *joking*, Ron," said Kim.

Ron blinked. It took him a moment to catch up. "Good one, good one," he finally said with a forced laugh. "So . . . did Kim tell you *I'm* her sidekick? 'Cause that role's *definitely* taken . . . by *me*."

"Right," Monique said as she stood up. "Well, you know, I'd better get to class. Later, Kim. Um . . . nice meeting you, Ron."

"Likewise, I'm sure," Ron replied.

When Monique was gone, Kim turned to Ron. "What is your problem?" she demanded. "You're acting really weird."

"Well, let's see," said Ron. "You went to the museum with Monique. Not me. Monique was with you this morning. Not me. Hmmmm . . . pattern?"

"Yeah, you being weird!" Kim replied.

"No. We're drifting apart because you're excluding me," Ron said.

"I am not excluding you," said Kim. "It's just that you and Monique are . . . different."

"Oh, now you're going to tell me that sometimes growing up means growing apart. I've heard it before, Kim." Ron paused to wipe away a tear. "Billy Bawlwiki, second grade."

"You are so blowing this out of proportion," Kim said as she placed her hand on her head.

"Okay, maybe I am," Ron said, sighing. "Ooooh, don't forget"—Ron whipped out the wrestling tickets—"Mayhem in Middleton! Tonight."

"Those tickets are for you," Kim replied. "I kind of already made plans with . . . uh . . . Monique."

There was heavy silence for a moment. Then Ron frowned. "I blame the smoothies," he said.

He leaped to his feet and tossed the tickets on the table. "Here," he said. "Jackie gave these to you."

"And I gave them to *you*," Kim replied.

"And I'm giving 'em back to *you*!" Ron cried. Then he snatched one of the tickets back. "Except this one," he added. "But only because it'll be the highlight of my life."

He turned and walked away.

"Ron!" Kim cried. But he was already gone.

CHAPTER 7

OUTSIDE THE LOCAL ARENA, WRES-TLING FANS WERE LINING UP AT THE GATES WEARING THEIR GWA OFFI-CIAL GEAR. They couldn't wait for Mayhem in Middleton to start!

Backstage, Pain King and Steel Toe were in their dressing room, preparing for the big event.

"So," said Pain King in a slightly bored tone as he tied his shoe, "are you taking a vacation this year?"

"Yeah, we went ahead and rented a cottage out on Martha's Vineyard," Steel Toe replied. "You know, it will be nice to get a chance to relax with the wife and kids."

Pain King nodded and placed his crown on his head. "Sounds charming."

Just then, someone knocked at the door. The two wrestlers jumped to their feet and angrily waved their fists at each other.

"I hate your guts!" shouted Pain King.

"I'm taking you down, slime," barked Steel Toe as he pointed his finger in Pain King's face.

The door opened and in walked Jackie Oaks.

Pain King relaxed. "Oh, Jackie, phew," he said, wiping the sweat from his forehead.

"Man," said Steel Toe, "I thought you were a reporter or something!"

"Hey, listen," Jackie said. "What do you guys think about me getting into the ring with you tonight, huh?" He stood as tall as he could.

Steel Toe and Pain King looked down at the promoter—and burst into laughter.

"C'mon, Jackie. Be reasonable," said Pain King.

"Yeah," Steel Toe added. "I don't mean to sell you short—oops—"

Jackie glared. "Very funny, very funny, yeah," he snapped.

"Sorry, man, I didn't mean it like that," said Steel Toe sincerely.

Pain King patted Jackie Oaks on the back. "Stick

to promoting, Jackie," he said. "That's what you're good at."

Jackie frowned and left the dressing room. Out in the hall, he reached into his pocket and pulled out a golden chain with something shaped like a half-moon hanging from it. It was Cleopatra's enchanted talisman!

"Ah," said Jackie with an evil grin. "This is all going to change . . . tonight!"

Meanwhile, near center stage, Ron Stoppable waved at two big guys sitting in the front row.

"Hey! Nice seats!" Ron called.

"Yeah, definitely!" one of the guys boasted.

Then Ron waved his own ticket under their noses. "But not as nice as mine!" he boasted right back. "*Backstage*, baby!"

Ron and Rufus slapped a high five as they reached the stage curtain.

"Gonna see my man Steel Toe," said Ron as he flashed his pass to the bored security guard.

The guard grunted and pulled the curtain aside.

Ron and Rufus wandered backstage, taking in all the sights, sounds, and smells of GWA—up close and personal.

Ron spotted Pain King and his hero, Steel Toe.

"It's Steel Toe! And Pain King!" he squealed. "So close I could touch them! But I won't," he decided. "Because I'm *cool*. Yo, Steel Toe. 'Sup, Pain?" he said.

Then Ron just couldn't help himself. He reached out and patted Steel Toe on the back. Even Rufus put his little paw out.

"I touched Steel Toe!" Ron cried.

Steel Toe stared at Ron and then Rufus. "Your gerbil's totally bald, man," he said.

Ron was giddy. His wrestling hero had actually *talked* to him. "Yes! Thank you!" he cried. Then Ron totally lost it. *Forget cool,* he thought. *I want to remember this moment forever!* He pulled up his shirt and exposed his belly. "Could I have an autograph?" he asked. "Could you make it to, um, to Ron?"

"Uh, sure. Let me get a pen," said Pain King, thinking Ron was asking for *his* autograph. He turned and yelled for his promoter. "Yo, Jackie!"

"Yeah," said Steel Toe, looking around. "Where is that guy? I need my sunglasses, pronto."

"I'll get them!" Ron offered to his hero. "Can I? Please? Please? Please?"

Steel Toe nodded. "Sure, kid. They're in my dressing room."

Ron rushed to the dressing room. Little did he know that in that very room, a strange ritual was underway.

Candles burned all around. The smell of incense filled the room. In the center of the space stood Jackie Oaks. But instead of his usual silk suit, Jackie wore Egyptian garb and sandals. Around his neck hung the talisman of Cleopatra.

"All right, let me see if I've got everything," Jackie mumbled as he studied his to-do list. "Open-toed sandals, check. Talisman—oh, it's glowing. That is nice, uh, beautiful, yeah."

Then Jackie took from his costume another list. This one was older—much, *much* older. It was written on a piece of cracked and yellowed parchment.

"My ancient papyrus," Jackie continued, "which I shall now read from—'Anubis, protector of the tomb, your time is now the time of doom.'"

As he chanted the magic words, an eerie wind blew through the dressing room.

Then Jackie's eyes began to glow yellow. His muscles bulged. His teeth became fangs. His ears grew into points, and his nose lengthened into a long snout. He was transformed into an eight-foot giant with a jackal head!

Ron stood at the open door, his mouth gaping. Rufus let out a frightened squeal and buried himself in Ron's pocket. The *thing* that was Jackie Oaks turned to face Ron, teeth bared in a bestial snarl.

"You know what?" Ron whimpered. "I can just come back later." Instantly, the jackal-headed creature snatched him up. With a savage roar, the monster threw Ron out of the dressing room.

Ron hurtled through the air and struck a food-service cart. Sandwiches flew everywhere. A quivering Rufus jumped out of Ron's pocket and hid under a piece of lettuce.

"You want to be left alone. I'm down with that," Ron told the creature.

Still growing, the jackal-headed giant burst out of the dressing room, roared once again, and shook his mighty fists at the ceiling. He stomped toward Ron and Rufus.

"Tonight," he roared, "the world will see the fearsome power of . . . the Jackal!"

CHAPTER 8

THE JACKAL, NOW TEN FEET TALL AND STILL GROWING, GRABBED RON IN ONE MAMMOTH PAW.

"I've seen!" Ron howled. "I believe!"

Laughing evilly, the Jackal hurled Ron down the hall and through the curtains. Yelling, Ron sailed over the crowded arena and slammed right into Steel Toe, just as he was about to grapple with Pain King.

Steel Toe went down. The crowd jumped to its feet and booed Ron.

Pain King grabbed Ron by the shoulders and shook him. "What are you doing?" he cried.

Ron pointed to the opposite end of the ring. "Uh, there's a problem," he said weakly. "Him!"

Pain King stared in disbelief as the glowing ten-foot-tall figure of the Jackal stepped over the ropes and into the ring. The Jackal punched his fist into his hand and ground it down. He was ready for a fight!

Meanwhile, far away from the mayhem, Kim was sitting with Monique at Middleton's most popular coffeehouse. People were sipping hot beverages, reading books, and relaxing. There was certainly no mayhem in sight.

Monique was in a good mood, but she could see that Kim wasn't. "Not enough froth in your latte?" Monique asked.

"No," Kim sighed. "I'm just feeling guilty. I kind of blew off Ron to be here tonight."

"Why didn't you bring him along?" Monique asked.

"Unless someone put a waiter in a headlock, this is definitely *not* Ron's scene," she said. "Besides, he had a date with Steel Toe."

"He scored tickets to Mayhem in Middleton?" Monique exclaimed. "The GWA rocks!" She threw a few excited punches into the air.

"What?" cried Kim.

"Pretty tacky, I know," Monique confessed. "But I absolutely love it. Pain King's my boy."

Kim slapped her forehead. "I can't believe you and Ron have something in common."

Just then, Kim's Kimmunicator chirped and she tapped it. A hologram of Wade appeared before her. "What up, Wade?" she asked casually.

"More on that talisman," Wade replied. "If the holder recites an incantation from an ancient text, the spirit of Anubis could actually control him."

"Sounds bad," said Kim.

"Very," Wade assured her.

"So, we'd better find that ancient text," Kim noted.

"Too late," said Wade. "Somebody already found it. Some masked guy stole it from the university in Chicago."

Kim nodded. "Do you have access to the police report?"

Wade tapped some keys and the report appeared on the hologram.

"The thief was super short!" said Kim, looking at a photo in the report. "And the GWA was in Chicago before Middleton!"

That clinched it! Kim had to go before it was too late. She jumped up and grabbed her backpack.

"Sorry, Monique," Kim said. "I keep running out on you. Rain check?"

At Middleton Arena, the Jackal stood in the center of the ring.

"Who is this guy?" Pain King asked.

"Man, beats me," said Steel Toe.

"It's Jackie," Ron told them. "He's got supernatural powers!"

"Jackie Oaks?" said a surprised Pain King.

"You all said I was too small to get in the ring!" roared the Jackal. "Well, here I am! You still think I'm too small?"

Then the Jackal reached out and grabbed a wrestler in each gigantic paw—and the crowd went wild!

"The Jackal's awesome!" the guys in the front row cried.

Boldly, Ron walked right up to the Jackal and commanded, "You made your point, Jackie. Now put them down!"

"I am no longer Jackie!" the creature roared. "I am now . . . the Jackal!"

Then the monster fired glowing bolts of power from his eyes. The beams struck Ron and sent him flying across the ring and into the ropes.

Yikes! Takedown!

CHAPTER 9

KIM POSSIBLE DASHED INTO THE ARENA AND FORCED HER WAY THROUGH THE MOB. "Excuse me. Pardon me. . . . Excuse me, I'm gonna squeeze through here," she said politely. Finally, Kim decided she had no time for manners.

"Out of my way!" she yelled. The crowd parted and Kim rushed to the ring in time to see Ron break down completely.

"First I lose my best friend, now professional wrestling! Everything's ruined," Ron sobbed.

"You didn't lose your best friend," said Kim.

"KP?" said Ron.

"And don't worry," said a determined Kim

Possible. "We're going to save this . . . this . . . uh . . . would you call it a *sport*?"

Ron jumped to his feet. "The most excellent one ever," he declared.

"Ron, are you okay?" Kim asked.

"Kim!" Ron cried, a new realization hitting him. "You decided to use your ticket!"

"I think Jackie is the museum thief," Kim told Ron.

"Old news," Ron replied. "The question is, what now?"

Kim jumped over the ropes and into the ring. "Let's take him down!" she declared.

Ron and Kim gave each other a high five.

"I'd tag team with you any day, KP!" said Ron.

"This'll be easy," said Kim. She believed it, too. Until she saw the Jackal twirl Pain King and Steel Toe like a pair of batons!

The Jackal released the wrestlers and they flew into the ropes, bouncing off and slamming into each other in the center of the ring.

"I will take on all comers in a no-holds-barred grudge match. Right here! Right now!" the Jackal declared.

The Jackal gazed out at the crowd. Then he

fired twin bolts of fire from his eyes. The fire incinerated a tub of popcorn that a fan in the stands was holding.

"Awesome rocket effects, bro!" shouted the fan.

Then the Jackal shot green electric bolts of energy from his hands. They destroyed a banner hanging nearby. But he wasn't done yet. He moved his hands in a motion that cause a tornado to form. Soon it consumed every object that wasn't bolted down in the arena.

"Prepare to be body-slammered, Jackal," said Kim through the wind and debris.

"That's body-*slammed*," Ron said. "Better let me do it."

Ron grabbed the Jackal's leg, but the creature kicked him away as if he were a fly. Ron landed on the ropes with a thud.

"You go," Ron told Kim.

Kim looked up at the Jackal. "Why don't you try it *without* the talisman?" she taunted.

"Why don't you try and make me?" roared the Jackal. With a wave of his hand, he made Kim float up into the air. "I am all-powerful," he declared. Then he let Kim drop to the mat.

"Ouch!" said Kim.

As Ron rushed to help her, Kim's eyes narrowed at the jackal-headed jerk. "You distract him. I'll go for the talisman," she told Ron.

Ron gave her a thumbs-up. "Distraction. Solid!" he cried.

Ron strode boldly up to the creature.

"Steel Toe's number one!" Ron yelled. "Jackal who? Jackal who? Steel Toe's number one!"

The Jackal spun on Ron with a growl.

"That's right, you heard me," said Ron.

As the Jackal stalked forward, Kim climbed the ropes behind the creature. With a leap she landed right on the Jackal's back. Kim reached over his shoulder and grabbed for the talisman. But the Jackal snatched Kim off his back and hurled her toward the ropes.

"Whaa!" cried Kim.

"From now on, the world will bow down to *me*!" roared the Jackal. Then he leaped over the ropes and into the panicked crowd. Fans scattered as the Jackal smashed seats and threw them aside.

Kim jumped to her feet. "As long as he has that talisman on, this guy can't be stopped," she said. "Ron, you keep the Jackal busy."

"I did that already!" Ron cried. "And I have the rope burns to show for it."

"Doesn't have to be for long," said Kim. She pointed to Pain King and Steel Toe. "Get them to help."

Ron ran up to the wrestlers. "We've got to keep the Jackal busy!" he cried.

But the wrestlers shook their heads. They were still recovering from their last encounter with the Jackal. "No way, man!" Pain King replied. "The guy is scary."

"There's no way," said Steel Toe. "I don't want a piece of this guy. Did you see his eyes? They're glowing!"

"Gentlemen," said Ron. "You are not just enter-tainers. You are not just gifted athletes. You're heroes!"

Steel Toe and Pain King exchanged glances, then smiled. Ron was right. "Let's get it on!" the wrestlers cried together. Then they challenged the Jackal. With a roar, the creature turned toward Steel Toe and Pain King and leaped back into the ring to face them. Even Ron helped out, although he was quickly flung back into the ropes again.

Above them on a catwalk, Kim smiled. With the Jackal back in the ring, she quickly attached her grappling hook to the catwalk. Then she grabbed the cable and swung over the side!

As the Jackal knocked the two wrestlers around, Kim swung by him and tried to grab the talisman. She got a nasty surprise when beams from the Jackal's glowing eyes cut the cable in two. Down she plunged!

Kim spun in the air and bounced on the wrestling ring's ropes. She flew over the Jackal's head to the other side of the ring—but she couldn't grab the talisman!

Ron pulled Rufus out of his pocket and aimed the mole rat at the Jackal.

"One chance, buddy!" Ron cried. Rufus knew it was up to him. He gave Ron a nod. Then Ron hurled Rufus through the air!

"Noooo!" bellowed the Jackal as Rufus snatched the talisman from his neck and continued flying past.

"Gotcha, Rufus!" Kim cried when she caught the flying mole rat.

A wind blew through the arena, whirling around the Jackal, who suddenly shrank in size. The jackal head disappeared. A moment later, Jackie Oaks stood in the center of the ring, staring up at a very angry Pain King and Steel Toe.

"Um, ha, ha, guys," whined Jackie. "Be reasonable."

But Pain King snatched Jackie up and twirled the helpless promoter over his head.

"Jackie, you're going down!" Pain King cried. Then he hurled Jackie into the audience.

Kim, Ron, Rufus, and the wrestlers waved as the crowd went wild! "Dude, that's the best, most awesome, most totally rippin' show I've ever seen," cried one fan.

"No way, man!" yelled another fan. "The whole Jackal thing was totally fake!"

CHAPTER 10

THE NEXT DAY, KIM, RON, AND MONIQUE SAT IN A BOOTH AT BUENO NACHO. Each had a plate of burritos in front of them.

"You know," said Monique, "I still can't believe you met Pain King and Steel Toe."

"I can't believe you're into wrestling," said Ron.

Kim rolled her eyes. "I can't believe I know either of you," she groaned.

"Enough talk!" Monique cried, lifting her burrito. Then she challenged Ron to an eating contest. "In the famous words of Pain King, *you're going down*!" said Monique.

"Au contraire," Ron replied, raising his burrito. "It is you who will be going down."

Ron and Monique stared at each other, burritos at the ready.

"First one to drip is the loser," Monique declared.

"Better get your bib, baby," Ron said, laughing.

"So wrong!" cried Monique.

Rufus hopped onto the table and raised a napkin to signal the start of the contest. He dramatically dropped the napkin. The contest had begun!

As Ron and Monique began gobbling up their burritos, Kim looked on in disbelief. Then she shrugged. "I think this is the beginning of a very weird friendship," she said with a laugh.

MIDDLETON MATTERS

Middle-of-the-Road News

MIDDLETON HAPPENINGS

This week in Middleton, there are family-friendly events for every resident to enjoy—whether you're a wrestling fanatic, a history buff, a chic fashionista, or someone with a very specific interest in Egyptian talismans!

First up, the Global Wrestling Association, known as the GWA, is in town presenting Mayhem in Middleton, a match that features two of wrestling's biggest rivals: Pain King and Steel Toe. Jackie Oaks, founder of the GWA, had this to yell: "Are you ready for head-bumping, chest-thumping, back-breaking, ground-shaking con-fron-ta-tion?" The first hundred fans not to be trampled get a free GWA tour T-shirt. The GWA legal team kindly reminds attendees not to look directly into Pain King's bionic eye, as it may cause permanent damage.

If wrestling isn't your cup of tea, the Middleton Art Museum will be opening a new exhibit called Cleopatra's Closet, which features many artifacts from Cleopatra's era. Items on view range from jewelry, mosaics, and sculptures to ancient talismans that once were thought to hold mysterious powers. In partnership with the museum, Club Banana will be hosting a special preview of the exhibit for Club Banana frequent buyers. They also will be debuting a new line of ancient-Egyptian-inspired styles.

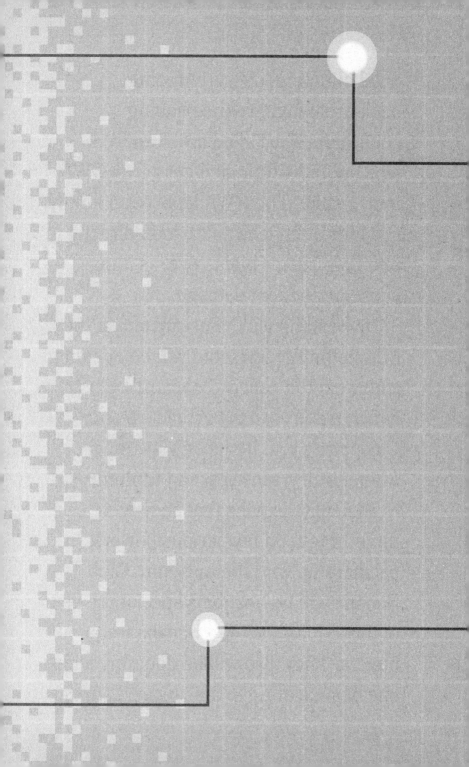

Notes for Mission #4143

Last week our martial arts club fundraiser was a bit of a dud, and now we're dangerously low on funds. Let's just say people weren't very excited to purchase a piece of wood, even if they could karate-chop it with their own hand. I just need to find some time to think about a new fundraiser. Monogrammed nunchucks? Collapsible bo staffs? I'll have to see if any of the other club members have ideas.

Recently, I've been doing some online research about the GJN, or Global Justice Network. Not that I would ever want to join, but sometimes crime fighting can get, well, a little lonely. Plus, GJN agents work with some major budgets. Every agent gets a standard-issue GJN computer complete with mobile database, hovercraft, and stun watch. Also, I would love to meet the head of GJN, Dr. Director. She has a really impressive background, and I think I could learn a lot from her.

Who knows if I'll ever meet her, though; the GJN is so secretive no one knows how to get to its headquarters. If you are invited for a visit, the GJN finds you, opens a hole in the sidewalk, and sucks you down a complex tunnel system so its headquarters location remains top secret.

That reminds me, strange reports of large patches of grass appearing on concrete sidewalks have been coming out of Tokyo. The only other report of this type of activity happened a while back when a new grass-covered island popped up in the middle of the ocean. Could the Tokyo situation be a test for a much larger plan?

Name: *Duff Killigan*

Wanted For: Trying to turn the world into his golf course

Strength: Use of explosive golf balls

Weakness: All other sports besides golf

Last Seen: On a golf course in southern Florida

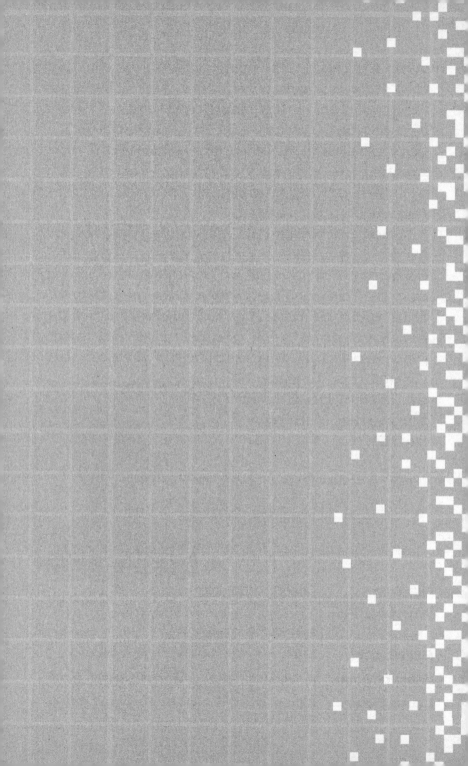

CHAPTER 1

SAVING THE WORLD WITHOUT A DRIVER'S LICENSE? *No big,* thought Kim Possible. But this?

This was a challenge. This was martial arts competition practice!

As Kim struggled to finish the final move in her routine, Bonnie Rockwaller walked in, late as usual. Bonnie was the newest member of the Martial Arts Club. She didn't seem to practice much, but Kim knew Bonnie well enough to know she needed to keep an eye on her.

"Great spin kick, Tara!" Kim cheered on her talented teammate. With the martial arts regional competition in a few days, the club had been practicing a lot during the week. As co-captain, Kim needed to make sure her teammates were still motivated.

"Okay. Great practice, team!" Kim called to her fellow Martial Arts Club members. The group gathered their things and filed out of the Middleton High gym.

"Kim . . . can we chat?" Bonnie said in her usual sweet-and-sour way. Bonnie was Kim's rival. She was also perfect—in her own mind!

Kim was *so* not looking forward to dealing with Bonnie. But Kim was team co-captain. So she forced herself to face Bonnie and say, "Sure, Bonnie. I have time for anyone in the Martial Arts Club. What's your ish?"

Bonnie took Kim by the arm. "Well, it's really *your* ish. You seem . . . tired."

"I did fly in from Abu Dhabi this morning. Rescued an ambassador," Kim said proudly.

"Which is nice. But you've gotta ask yourself: did you give the club one hundred and ten percent today?"

"One hundred and *twenty* percent, Bonnie," Kim said, getting a little upset at Bonnie's nasty tone.

"I happen to think the club deserves a captain

who gives, like . . . one hundred and *thirty* percent," Bonnie said smugly.

Kim was starting to get the picture. "Someone like—"

"Me," Bonnie said, pointing to herself.

"Look, if you want to make a play for my spot as captain, take it to the club," Kim said. "If they want Bonnie instead of Kim, super for Bonnie."

"Go ahead, be little Miss Smug-Mug, but I *will* be club captain," Bonnie snapped.

Kim fumed. Fighting supervillains really *was* no big compared with a high school headache like this!

After practice, Kim found her best friend, Ron Stoppable, at their usual after-school hangout, Bueno Nacho.

"I can't believe this," Kim said in one long groan.

"Believe it, KP. They're cutting back on the beans." Ron squinted at his burrito.

Kim sighed. She was talking about *Bonnie*, not burritos. Sitting in the booth across from Ron, she waited for him to get serious.

Ron reached into his pocket and pulled out his

pet naked mole rat. Rufus, half asleep, gave a big yawn.

"Rufus," Ron said, "I want an analysis of this burrito. Stat!"

Rufus's eyes popped open. *Mmm-yummmmmm.* He licked his lips.

"Nothing invasive," Ron told him. "Just take a look around. I want a cheese-to-bean ratio."

Rufus gave Ron a thumbs-up. Then he lifted up the tortilla with his paw and crawled inside the tasty burrito.

Kim drummed her fingers on the table. This was *not* the kind of serious talk she'd had in mind when she sat down. "Ron, have you been listening to a word I've said?"

Ron straightened up and did his best Kim Possible impersonation: "'Bonnie has the nerve to challenge me after all I've done for the club? After all I've done for her! I can't believe this.' Close quote."

Kim took an annoyed slurp of soda. Ron had gotten her good. Talk about Humiliation Nation!

"Now," he said, "were *you* listening to *my* burrito problem?"

A huge burp ripped through Bueno Nacho. Ron looked down to see where the burp had come from.

"Hey!" Ron cried.

Rufus's belly was bulging out. The naked mole rat gave Ron a thumbs-up. So much for a noninvasive scan . . . Rufus had eaten the entire burrito! Rufus groaned and fell back on the plastic tray, his little tongue hanging from his little mouth. He was in a total food coma.

Ron ordered another burrito. After he had finished gulping it down, Kim and Ron left the restaurant, and Kim continued talking about the *real* problem: Bonnie Rockwaller.

"Bonnie's just wasting her time," Kim said. "She doesn't stand a chance."

"Be careful, Kim. She's tricky," Ron said as he walked ahead of her. "Expect it to get dirty."

Suddenly, a hole in the ground opened up right below where Kim was walking. *Whoosh!* Kim fell through, and just as suddenly, the hole closed again.

Ron heard Kim cry out. He looked all around, completely confused. "Kim?" he asked. But no one answered. She was gone.

CHAPTER 2

PLOP! Kim dropped from the mysterious hole in the sidewalk. She found herself trapped inside a strange glass capsule just big enough for her to fit inside. As she got to her feet, she heard a door shut above her.

"Hey!" she yelled, knocking on the glass enclosure.

Swoosh! The tiny glass capsule dropped like a speeding elevator. It carried her underground through a maze of green tubes. *Zig!* Her tube turned to the right. *Zag!* It turned to the left. *Whoosh!* It did a loop-the-loop—then it zoomed straight down. It was traveling so fast that the bottom started flaming!

Finally, it stopped with a thud. And Kim was *not* happy.

"Let me out!" Kim pounded on the glass walls. "Let me"—suddenly, the glass in front of her slid open—"out!"

She tumbled free, landing face-first on the dirt floor.

"Okay . . ." she said, looking all around, "what's the sitch?"

Suddenly, she saw a pair of tall black boots in front of her. She looked up and saw a woman with an eye patch. "Kim Possible. Welcome."

Kim didn't recognize the woman. She had short dark hair and wore a skintight blue uniform with long sleeves.

"Welcome to where?" Kim asked as she stood up.

"To the Global Justice Network," said the woman as she lightly shook Kim's hand.

"GJN? No way!" Kim couldn't believe it. She'd always admired their crime-fighting work. As her eyes adjusted to the darkness, she saw a team monitoring computers and others walking briskly to handle important crime-fighting stuff.

"Affirmative way," said the woman. "I'm Dr. Director, the head of GJN."

Whoosh! Kim spun around to see another green tube arrive and open. Out walked a boy. He definitely didn't have the crash-landing Kim had moments before. He was Kim's age and dressed in a blue uniform like Dr. Director's. He would have seemed friendly if the look on his face hadn't been so serious. He strode over to Kim and Dr. Director.

"This is Will Du, our *number one* agent," said Dr. Director. Then to both of them she said, "Follow me."

The two teenagers stared at each other. Will raised an eyebrow, and Kim breezed past, thinking, *Who* is *this guy and what's* his *ish?*

Kim and Will Du sat down next to Dr. Director at a huge round table with over thirty seats. Three huge projector screens hung above them.

"This is Professor Sylvan Green," said Dr. Director, flicking a button on a remote control. An image of the professor flashed on all three screens. He was a gawky young man with big ears, sandy brown hair, and glasses.

The head of GJN continued: "In the 1960s he developed a top-secret missile defense project."

"The Sirenita guided-missile tracking system," Kim said.

Dr. Director looked shocked—that was top-secret stuff! "Where did you get that information?"

Kim shrugged. "Online."

"Oh. Ah." Dr. Director cleared her throat. She continued with another click of the remote.

"This is Professor Green, currently." A new image showed a man with the same glasses and the same big ears. Only now his hair was gone, and he was riding on a lawn mower. "Retired. Place of residence: Florida."

"But now he's disappeared," Kim said.

Dr. Director sighed. "Yes. Was that on the Internet, too?"

"No," Kim told her. "That was a guess."

"Kim," said Dr. Director, "what would you say to helping Agent Du find Professor Green?"

Kim glanced at Agent Will Du. He looked like he'd be about as much fun as cleaning her room. "Does Agent Du talk?"

"Fourteen languages. Thirty-two regional dialects," Agent Du responded quickly.

"That's cool. I'm taking French class right now." Kim turned to Dr. Director. "Ah, you know, this is a ferociously bad time for me. There's this girl at school, a major 'all that' type, and really I—"

"Dr. Director, permission to speak freely," Will said, scowling.

"Granted," his boss said.

"This is an insult!" Will cried. "I am a highly trained professional. And she's . . . she's . . . an *amateur*!"

First Bonnie, now this guy, Kim thought, annoyed. Challenges were piling up everywhere!

"Okay. I'm in," she told them, narrowing her eyes.

Will Du sneered. But he didn't say another word.

Dr. Director smiled. "Kim Possible, Agent Du . . . good luck."

They were certainly going to need it.

CHAPTER 3

"MAN, I THOUGHT FOR SURE BONNIE HAD TAKEN YOU OUT OF THE PICTURE," RON SAID TO KIM AFTER SCHOOL THE NEXT DAY. They were walking out the front entrance of Middleton High.

"Oh, please," Kim said. "You know, she didn't even show up for practice. Typical Bonnie."

"Miss Possible . . ." Kim and Ron stopped when they heard the unfriendly voice. It was Will Du, who had just appeared on the sidewalk in front of them. "Are you ready to assist me in *my* investigation?" he asked smugly.

"*Assist* you? No," Kim told him. "*Work with you as an equal?* Sure."

Ron thought he'd better check out this Will Du

dude. He decided to start with the friendly approach. "Yoha-broha!" he said with a wave of his hand.

Agent Du reacted like he was being attacked. He tapped a button on the face of his watch. A wire shot out of the timepiece and attached itself to Ron's chest.

Zappo! An electric shock ran through Ron. His hair stood up straight from his head before he collapsed in a heap.

Kim rushed over to help. She yelled at Will, "What did you do to him?"

"Stopwatch stun prong. Temporary paralysis," Will said with total calm. "Standard procedure for any unknown person who comes within one meter of my person."

Rufus crawled up onto Ron's shoulder, looking queasy.

"Oh, poor Rufus," Kim said.

Now Agent Du began to talk into his watch. Apparently, it was also a voice recorder. "Note: subject appears to carry hairless rodent everywhere."

This boy was getting Kim totally tweaked. She waved Rufus by his tail right in Will's face. "His name is Rufus, and he's a naked mole rat, Mr. I-Know-Everything."

"Ahhh . . . *Heterocephalus glaber,*" Will babbled into his watch.

"Latin, big deal," Kim replied, not impressed.

Ron sprang to his feet, wide-awake. Time for take two. "Yoha-broha!" he said again, reaching out his hand for a handshake.

Will jumped back into a martial arts pose.

"*Wha-ha!*" Ron's arms flew wildly around. He cracked his neck. "Right back atcha, dude!" he cried.

Kim placed Rufus's frozen tail into Ron's fist. "Come on, you two."

As she moved past the boys, who were still holding their martial arts poses, Kim saw Bonnie Rockwaller walking toward her.

"Hi, K," Bonnie sang with totally fake cheeriness.

"Missed you at practice, B," Kim sang right back, folding her arms.

"I had to launch our new fund-raiser," Bonnie said as she handed Kim a purple box with a ribbon.

Kim looked at the strange box in her hands. "What fund-raiser?"

"I know your *world saving* keeps you busy and all," Bonnie said. "But do you think maybe *you* can sell a box?"

"Oh, chocolates." Kim pulled out a bar. "Oh, I could sell a box. Easy."

"Super!" Bonnie said.

Just then, a horn blared loudly from the school parking lot. Bonnie turned and walked over to a huge tractor trailer. It was filled with chocolate bars!

"Hoping to sell a few myself," said Bonnie.

A few? thought Kim. There must have been *thousands* of bars in there!

Bonnie hopped into the truck. "Later," she said. Then the huge candy rig drove off.

"You know, she's only kidding herself," Kim said to Ron and Will. "There is no way she's gonna sell all that. Let's just get on with the mission."

Ron grabbed her by the arm. "Wait, KP. Am I the only one taking the Bonnie problem seriously?"

Kim waved her hand like *whatever.* "Oh, the Bonnie problem is really no big."

"Kim, we cannot ignore the chocolate challenge," Ron said seriously.

"We?" she asked.

"I'm here for you. Use me," said Ron.

"As what?" asked Kim.

He grabbed the candy box from her. "I am a

natural-born seller. I have the gift of gab. Here, allow me to demonstrate."

This, Kim thought, she would *have* to see. Salesman Stoppable walked up to Will. Agent Du stood typically solid and unblinking. "Good day, sir," Ron began. "You look like a gentleman who enjoys the finer things in life. And what could be better than one point nine ounces of rich, creamy chocolate?"

Will just stared. Then he blinked once.

Ron continued his sales pitch. "I got plain? Crispy? Peanut?" He looked frantically in the box for the perfect bar to tempt Agent Will Du.

"Mac-a-da-mi-a," Ron teased, holding the candy bar under Will's nose. But Will still gave no response.

Ron stomped back over to Kim. "That's a bad example," he growled. "No one can sell to *that* guy."

Rufus grabbed a candy bar and scampered over to the grim agent.

Will stared at the naked mole rat. Then he handed over a dollar for the chocolate.

Waving the money in the air, Rufus squealed.

"Except him," said Ron with a shrug.

CHAPTER 4

LATER THAT AFTERNOON, KIM, RON, AND WILL WENT OVER TO KIM'S HOUSE TO DISCUSS THEIR MISSION.

They were sitting around the kitchen table, but the only item on the menu was strategy. Ron started drifting off, thinking about Bueno Nacho.

"Hi, Kimmy," said Kim's mom, walking into the kitchen. "Who's your new friend?"

Will jumped up from the kitchen table and bowed deeply. "Agent Will Du, ma'am. It's an honor to meet you, Dr. Possible."

Kim's mom put her hand to her chest in surprise. "You know me?"

"Your recent paper on the application of lasers in subcranial exploration was fascinating," Will said in his most respectful voice. "And the photograph did not do you justice."

Dr. Possible whispered to her daughter, "Invite him over more often."

Mothers! Kim thought. "Mom, I've got to find a missing scientist."

"Good luck, Kimmy," Dr. Possible said as she left the room. "Have fun, kids."

Kim tapped her Kimmunicator. It was like a cell phone, hologram, and supercomputer put together.

A hologram of her friend Wade's face appeared in front of her. Wade was the tech genius who helped Kim and Ron on all their world-saving missions.

"Wade, did you get the data?" Kim asked.

"Got it," Wade responded. "A three-dimensional simulation of the missing professor's home."

Within a few moments, Wade's face was replaced by the home simulation. The see-through hologram took over the entire table. It was like an entire house *inside* Kim's house!

"Cool!" Ron said. "Hey, Rufus, Wade's gone 3-D!"

Rufus hopped onto the table and started strolling through the holo-house, looking for a place to kick back. He found a comfy chair and jumped into the air, hoping to land on it. But *bam!* He landed on his naked-mole-rat rear instead.

Will sneered. He thought this was a waste of time. "I've already examined the crime scene," he snapped.

Kim snapped back, "I haven't. Wade, enlarge the point of entry."

The hologram dissolved all around Rufus, who cried out in shock. It then projected a close-up of the side of the house. A large hole was blasted in the wall!

"Explosive method of entry. What's that?" Kim pointed at a tiny white speck in the hologram.

"Can't tell," Wade said. "I'll isolate and enlarge." There was the sound of his fingers flying across the keyboard.

The white speck grew larger and floated above the table.

"Good," Kim said. "Now let's try to fill in the blanks."

"Running extrapolation routine." Wade's computer program drew a picture of what the white speck used to be.

It was a golf ball.

"A golf ball?" Ron asked.

"Professor Green was retired," Will added. "Many retired people golf."

Wade's face appeared before them again. Kim turned to him. "Wade, does Professor Green show up in any online discussion groups?"

"Oh, yeah." Wade read from his monitor. "Gardening, botany, experimental fertilizers. His lawn won the bluegrass ribbon three years in a row."

"While this has been . . . informative, I have some real crime solving to do," Will said as he stood up. "This conversation is pointless. The man was obviously captured for his weapon-system expertise."

"He was a weapons expert in the sixties," Kim said. "You could look up what he knows in the library."

Will headed for the door. "Working with an amateur is clearly a waste of my time," he said.

Kim smiled big. She knew something Will didn't. "I haven't even told you about the other trace element I detected at the scene."

Will stopped in his tracks. "What is it?"

"Hyperactic acid. An experimental fertilizer. Black market only." Kim winked at Ron. She knew she was one step ahead of Will.

Ron could see a plan coming together. "Sounds

like we need to visit the world headquarters for black-market gardening supplies," he said. Then he looked around, confused, and asked, "Which would be *where*?

"And may I suggest a quick stop at Bueno Nacho to fuel up?"

Kim and Will looked at Ron. That was a definite no.

CHAPTER 5

THE DESERT MARKETPLACE WAS DARK AND DUSTY. Clay pots lined the empty alley. The only light came from a shadowy café. Kim Possible stepped up to the entrance. Ron and Will followed.

"If it's illegal, they sell it here," Kim said in a low voice. The place reeked of danger.

Ron didn't recognize the scent. He whipped out a bunch of chocolate bars. "Forget sellers," he said. "We need buyers. Ya gotta move this merchandise if you're gonna keep up with Bonnie."

"Bonnie is *so* not a threat," Kim said dismissively. "C'mon."

The inside of the café smelled like strange spiced

coffee. Men in red fez hats sat on velvet pillows and talked in hushed voices. In the far corner, on the biggest pillow, sat the biggest man.

"That's Big Daddy Brotherson," Kim told the others. "Every deal that goes down has his fingerprints all over it."

"Those are some *big* fingers," Ron said as he watched the huge, sweaty man chew on some grapes and spit the seeds onto the floor.

Will Du pushed Kim and Ron aside. "Excuse me, amateurs." He marched boldly across the room.

"Are you Big Daddy?" Will asked.

The large man smiled a greasy smile. "That depends."

"I've got no time for games." Will held up his fist.

"That's too bad," Big Daddy said, rubbing his hands together. "I was going to suggest you and my friend play *thud*."

Will swallowed hard, then said, "Thud?"

Big Daddy clapped his big hands. He was still smiling.

Out of the shadows came the huge figure of a bouncer. Unlike Big Daddy, the bouncer was *not* smiling.

Kim watched as the bouncer bounced Will across

the room and through the window. He landed on the ground with a *thud!* "Ow," he whimpered.

Big Daddy chuckled. "I love that game," he said, admiring the Will-shaped hole in the window. Ron raced outside to make sure Will was okay, but Kim lingered in the room.

"And I love it when I find out what I need to know"—Kim stepped close to Big Daddy—"like, who's been in the market for hyperactic acid?"

Big Daddy frowned at Kim. "Miss, we have one rule in this establishment: client confidentiality."

Kim pulled out a fund-raiser candy bar and waved it under his nose. He licked his lips and inhaled deeply. Sweat began to pour from his forehead.

"Is that milk chocolate?" he asked. Kim could hear his stomach growl.

She sniffed the chocolate bar. "With chewy nougat," she answered with a sly smile.

Outside the café, Will and Ron waited for Kim. When she finally walked out, she struck a confident pose. "Duff Killigan," she said proudly.

Ron's eyes got big. "Who's that?"

Will pulled out his phone. "My GJN mobile database will tell us all about Killigan. Standard issue for all *top* agents."

Kim tapped her Kimmunicator. "Well, this is extra special. Just for me."

A hologram of Wade appeared in front of Kim. She immediately asked Wade to grab all the latest information on Duff Killigan. Soon Wade's face was replaced with the information on Killigan.

Meanwhile, Will furiously pushed buttons on his device. They began reading the info as soon as it appeared before them. The data duel was on!

Kim read off a report: "'Duff Killigan. Born: Scotland.'"

"Former professional golfer," Will shot back.

Ron noticed a man standing on a nearby rooftop. The bright moon was shining behind him, so it was difficult to see his face. He looked like he was holding a golf club. That was strange, since Ron was pretty sure golf was more of a daytime sport.

"Ah . . . guys?" Ron said.

Will ignored Ron. "Banned from every golf course in the world. Even miniature golf."

"For excessive displays of temper," Kim countered, also ignoring Ron as newspaper articles flashed before her.

With a swing of his club, the golfer on the roof smacked a ball straight toward them.

"Fore!" the man yelled, and his voice echoed through the alley.

Ron yelled, "Guys!"

But Kim and Will were too busy data dueling.

"Weapon of choice—" Kim started.

"Exploding golf balls," Will finished.

Plop! The golf ball landed at their feet. Kim noticed that this particular golf ball was making a noise.

Beep, beep, beep, then (unfortunately) . . .

KABOOM!

CHAPTER 6

LUCKILY, JUST BEFORE THE GOLF BALL EXPLODED, RON PULLED KIM AND WILL TO SAFETY IN AN ALLEY.

Suddenly, Ron had a moment of panic. Where was his little naked whiskered friend? "Rufus, you okay?" he asked, pulling up the flap of his pants pocket.

Out popped the naked mole rat, a chocolate bar in his paw. He was more than okay. *Chomp!*

"Hey!" Ron cried, spying the chocolate. "You're paying for that!"

Suddenly, Will Du had a bright idea. "It all fits. The exploded golf ball at the crime scene. The attack on us. Killigan's our man."

"Gee, ya think?" Kim said. She rolled her eyes and tapped her Kimmunicator. "Wade, we're after a rogue golfer named Duff Killigan. We need a location on his lair."

"Did you say 'rogue golfer'?" Wade asked as his holographic face appeared before them.

"I know," Kim said. "Weird." She turned to Will and Ron. "Okay, I'm gonna go back to Middleton. See if Bonnie's sold any of *her* chocolate. Let's meet there in an hour."

Kim stood in the Middleton High gym. Her jaw almost dropped to the floor.

"You sold them all?" she asked, shocked.

Bonnie smiled. "To quote our previous club captain: 'No big.'"

"I'm not 'previous' yet," Kim snapped.

A bunch of the other members of the Martial Arts Club stepped up behind Bonnie.

"Thanks to Bonnie, we got new uniforms!" said Tara. "Aren't they badical?"

Bonnie tossed a new uniform in Kim's face. "Better suit up, Kim. We're working on our new routine."

"Don't tell me what to do," Kim said. "Wait, what new routine?"

"Mine," Bonnie said as she walked away.

Kim wrinkled her nose and said to herself, "Bonnie does not work this hard. She doesn't even have martial arts training. Something is up."

Meanwhile, Will and Ron were sitting in a booth at Bueno Nacho.

"Hey, Will, watch this," Ron said. He held up his burrito and squeezed. *Splursh!* The bean-and-cheese insides shot straight up in the air. Ron put his face under the falling food and caught it in one sloppy bite. *Glomp!*

"Pretty cool, huh?" Ron said.

"If by 'cool' you mean utterly repulsive," Will said with a frown, "then yes. Quite cool, indeed."

Rufus wanted to get in on the action. He stomped on a nacho chip. *Splursh!* The cheese went up in the air. *Glomp!* He caught it in his little mole-rat mouth.

"Nice one!" Ron said to Rufus, giving him a high five.

Will just stared at them.

"So, can I ask you a question?" said Ron.

"I'm pretty sure you can, considering your ability to speak in the English language." Will smirked while Ron stared at him blankly. He wasn't getting it. Will continued, "I believe you meant to say, '*May* I ask you a question.'"

"I'm not sure what you just said made any sense, but *may* I ask you a question? Wait, I guess this is my second question. May I ask you a second question?"

Will was growing increasingly annoyed. "If you must," he said with a huff.

"Do you do normal stuff? Like go to school?" Ron asked.

"I am tutored by some of the world's greatest minds," said Will proudly.

"Tutored, huh?" Ron said. "No shame in that. Even I needed a little extra help in math freshman year."

"It is not because I don't study," Will said.

"Dude, it's *cool*," said Ron.

"You obviously don't understand—"

Ron glanced at the clock. "Looks like it's time to meet Kim," he said.

"Sure, but just for the record, I'm a good student!" Will insisted, banging the table with his fists.

Back in the school's gym, Bonnie finished her new martial arts routine and flipped over to Kim. "In case you were wondering, Kim, that's what giving one hundred and *fifty* percent looks like."

"Careful there, Bonnie," Kim said, annoyed. "I hear when you hit one hundred and *sixty* percent, you spontaneously combust."

Ron and Will entered the gym.

Bonnie smiled. "Don't worry, Kim. *I'll* handle everything here. Just like a co-captain should."

Kim gritted her teeth. She was so upset Ron could almost see the steam coming out of her ears.

She tapped her Kimmunicator. "Wade, do you have an update on Duff Killigan's location?"

"Location confirmed," Wade responded with a thumbs-up.

She grabbed Ron by the shirt and stomped out. "Let's go," she grunted.

But even after Kim changed into her crime-fighting clothes, her mind was still on martial arts practice and the Bonnie situation.

"Bonnie is not this good. How could she have

come up with that routine? And did you see her flip over to me? What was with that?" she asked.

Ron grinned. "Somebody's upset," he said in a singsong.

"Am not," Kim snapped back—then she barked at the hologram of Wade. "Wade! We need a ride!"

"What upset *you*?" Wade asked calmly.

"I am *not* upset!" she barked again. *"Ride?"*

Suddenly, the sound of a sleek hover jet filled the air.

Kim was amazed to see their ride appear so fast. "Wade, how did you get—"

Then it dawned on Kim. "Oh," she groaned.

The ride was Agent Will Du's.

Beep! Beep! Standing next to Kim, Will waved a tiny remote control in her face. "The GJN hover jet," he bragged. "Standard issue for all *top* agents."

The jet floated close to the ground.

Cha-chung! Its metal door opened.

"Ladies first," Will said.

Kim fumed, her arms crossed. "Thanks," she said, trying to be nice. But what she was thinking was definitely *not* nice.

CHAPTER 7

THE HOVER JET ZOOMED ACROSS LAND AND SEA. Ron was the first to notice the tiny piece of rock entirely covered in grass, surrounded by dark crashing waves. He pointed out the window. "There it is . . . Killigan's Island."

In the middle of the island sat a huge, towering old castle. It was totally "evil lair" material. Will parked the hover jet, and they all headed for the castle's front door.

"Killigan must want Professor Green to build some kind of missile system," Will said as they entered the castle. A fire was roaring in the fireplace, which meant someone was definitely home. They needed to proceed with caution.

"I don't think so," Kim said, lowering her voice. "Green's *green thumb* is the key to this."

"Yeah, okay, now see that door?" Ron pointed to a mammoth wood door with old iron decorations at the far end of the castle hall. Torches burned on either side of it. "That just screams dungeon."

Both Will and Kim nodded. "Good call," they said.

As the three of them sneaked down the dimly lit stairs, Kim tried to put it all together: "Killigan captures Professor Green. Then he buys a ton of hyperactic acid. Which, by the way, Professor Green had been experimenting with at his home."

Suddenly, Kim remembered something Wade had told her about Green. "Award-winning lawn!"

Ron raised an eyebrow and said, "You mean, the dude's invented some sort of supergrass?"

Just then, they realized something strange about the dungeon. The walls, the tables, the chairs . . . *everything* was covered in grass.

Then they noticed something creeping toward them beneath the grass. When it got nearer, it wagged its tail. Then it barked.

"There's something you don't see every day," Ron said.

"Ron! Will! Quick!" Kim called from the other side of the dungeon. "I found Professor Green!"

Actually, what she found was more like a big, man-sized clump of grass. Kim addressed the grassy clump. "Professor Green, are you all right?"

All they could hear were muffled groans. They had to do something, and fast.

Ron jumped to the rescue. "Hang on!" he yelled as he pulled out Rufus, whose teeth started chomping. Ron moved Rufus over the grass like a pair of clippers. *Chomp! Chomp! Chomp!* Soon the professor was free.

"Oh, thank you," the old professor said, coughing out all manner of pollen. "Killigan trapped me in my own superfast-growing grass."

Kim gave Will an I-told-you-so smile and said, "Supergrass. Huh? Really?"

Will, who was *not* smiling, shoved Kim to the side. "Professor Green, I'm Agent Will Du. We need to debrief you on any weapons secrets that Killigan may have acquired."

The professor scratched his head. "Huh? Based on my work? Oh, Killigan could find out anything he wanted about my weapons work in a public library."

"Oh," said Will.

Score again! thought Kim.

Ron raised his hand and said, "Bonus question: what does Killigan want to do with the supergrass?"

"Oooh, oooh, I know, I know!" shouted someone with a Scottish accent. At the top of the dungeon stairs, Duff Killigan was waving his hand like a teacher's pet begging to be called on.

But it was Kim who gave the answer: "Duff Killigan is planning on covering the world in grass. To create one giant golf course."

"My own personal golf course, lassie," Killigan hollered. He wore a tiny green beret and a loud plaid kilt.

And plaid is so *last season,* thought Kim.

"That's insane," Will said.

Killigan leaned forward to taunt Agent Du. "Oooh, just see if you get a tee time." Then Killigan darted away.

Will charged up the stairs, hoping to get a piece of Killigan. All he got was a dungeon door slammed in his face. He tugged hard on the cold iron handle, but the door was locked shut.

Kim walked up to the struggling GJN agent. "Ah-uh-uh," she said. "*Ladies* first."

She plucked a lip gloss from her utility belt and

pulled off the cap. *Zzzz!* This was no ordinary lip gloss. It was a lip gloss laser!

Kim sliced through the iron lock with her laser beam. She kicked the door open.

"I knew you were good, lassie," Killigan said, leaning against his golf bag in the middle of the room.

Suddenly, Will charged at him. But the sneaky Scotsman swiped a club under Will's feet.

"*Him* I'm not so sure about—" Killigan said, watching Will trip across the room. He got tangled in a rug and landed in a heap, unconscious.

Kim carefully approached the villain. "Mr. Killigan, put down the golf clubs."

"You'll have to pry them out of my hands," said Killigan.

Out came another golf club. This time, Killigan started whacking golf balls all around the room.

"Fore!" he screamed.

Kim jumped up, grabbed the chandelier, and swung safely out of the way. Will wasn't so lucky. Just as he started to wake up . . . *Whap!* He got it in the head with a stray ball. Agent Du was down again.

"Aw! What a beautiful slice!" Killigan hopped up and kicked his heels in the air.

Kim flew down from the chandelier. She grabbed a pair of clubs from a wall ornament.

Killigan became furious. "You ruined my coat of arms."

Kim twirled the clubs in her hands like a martial arts master. She said, "I'll put back what belongs to you when you put back what belongs to Professor Green."

Killigan pulled out two clubs and mimicked Kim's twirling moves. "I cannot do it. I've got plans for that formula."

Clash! Kim's clubs cracked the tops off Killigan's weapons. He pulled out his last two irons. *Clang!* Kim knocked the clubs from Killigan's hands right in front of the fireplace.

"Oh, I'd love to play a round of sudden death," he said to her, "but I can't let the grass grow beneath my feet . . . yet." Killigan pushed a button on the fireplace, and a hole opened right below him. *Whoosh!* He fell through, and the hole closed again.

"Suddenly, the whole world is full of holes that people just whoosh away in!" Ron cried.

Will woke up. He rubbed his head.

Kim was already at the exit. "C'mon!" she called. "He's getting away!"

Outside, Kim pointed to the sky. "There he is!"

Will, Ron, and Professor Green all looked up. A huge blimp made of the same tacky plaid as Killigan's kilt floated away.

"We've got to get to the hover jet!" Will told the gang. Then, once again, he charged forward without thinking.

"Will! Wait!" Kim called as she, Ron, and the professor ran after him.

"What?" cried Will. "He's getting away."

"You've gotta be more careful," Kim warned Will. "Killigan probably has the place booby-trapped."

"Try *sand*-trapped," Ron said when he noticed that everyone was slowly sinking . . . into quicksand!

CHAPTER 8

KIM, RON, WILL, AND PROFESSOR GREEN SANK DEEPER AND DEEPER INTO THE QUICKSAND. They were up to their necks, with their arms trapped by their sides.

"Okay, whenever you two are ready," Ron said to Kim and Will.

"What are you talking about?" Will growled.

"You *both* have a plan," Ron explained. "So the sooner you guys fight over who has the *best* plan, the sooner we can get out of here."

"Your hover jet," Kim said to Will. "It must have a remote-command module or something!"

"Right. The RCM," Will said, still sinking.

Ron grinned and said, "Kim shoots. She scores!"

Then Ron turned to Will and asked, "So where is this RCM?"

Will frowned and said, "I, uh, left it in the hover jet."

Rufus, who was standing on Ron's head, put his face in his paws.

That gave Kim an idea. "*Rufus* won't sink in the quicksand," she said.

With a snappy salute, Rufus hopped lightly down and tiptoed across the sand's surface.

Kim smiled proudly at Will. "Oh, I am *so* in the zone."

Will wrinkled up his face. "Impressive . . . for an amateur."

A couple of minutes passed. Kim wished Rufus would hurry.

Ron began squirming in the sand. "This actually feels kinda nice," he said. He realized Professor Green hadn't said anything in a while. He turned to the professor to see he was covered in quicksand past his mouth. No wonder he hadn't said anything in a while—he couldn't! They had to act soon!

Finally, Ron's naked mole rat returned—with the RCM in his mouth.

Rufus spit the module at Will, who caught it in his teeth.

Through his clenched teeth, Will said, "Nice work, rodent." He chomped down on the RCM. *Beep! Beep!* The hover jet zoomed over to them. With another *beep! beep!* the hover jet dropped a rescue cable toward the quicksand.

"Ladies first," said Kim gleefully, making Will regret he'd ever used those teasing words with her.

As Kim was lifted out of the sand trap, Will said to Ron, "Why must she constantly irk me?"

"It's hard not to," Ron told him. "You're very irkable."

In no time, the hover jet was roaring through the air. Will was in the driver's seat. But his mind was not on driving. Instead, he turned all the way around to question Green. "Professor, did Killigan—"

Kim grabbed Will's head and turned him back to face the front. "You! Keep your eyes on the road."

With Will occupied, Ron decided to jump in. "So, Prof, any ideas about Killigan's target?"

"Oh, yes," Professor Green said, waving his arms as he talked. "He intends to strike at the first country where he was banned from a golf course—Japan."

CHAPTER 9

IN TOKYO, JAPAN, FRIGHTENED PEOPLE RAN THROUGH THE STREETS SCREAMING AS A TIDAL WAVE OF GRASS ROARED AFTER THEM.

Behind it all, the evil Duff Killigan was tossing Professor Green's fast-growing seeds everywhere. A couple of sprinkles from his watering can of black-market fertilizer and—*splort!*—the grass erupted from the ground like a spewing green volcano.

Killigan cackled madly. "It's pure dead brilliant!"

Will's hover jet arrived not a moment too soon. "Killigan! Stop!" Kim yelled, leaping to the ground.

"Nay! Not until the Pacific Rim is my driving range!" He threw seeds at Kim and drenched them with the supergrow liquid.

A huge surge of turf tumbled toward her. She jumped up and over the oncoming lawn. When she landed, it had already passed her by.

The hover jet was not so lucky. In a matter of seconds, the grass had completely covered the jet.

Inside, Will and Ron were trapped. Will pounded the dashboard and totally lost his cool. "Stupid, stupid Will," he chided himself.

"Play it off, dude," Ron said. "Kim can handle the grass man."

"No. Prepare to eject," Will said, and reached for the big red eject button.

But Ron was not prepared. "Wait, where do I sit, I mean . . ."

Punt! The ship ejected Will and Ron straight into the air, pushing them through the layer of grass. They flew right over the head of Duff Killigan.

Killigan ignored them. He was too busy driving a bunch of exploding golf balls at Kim. *Boom! Boom! Boom!*

A few yards away, Will landed coolly in a perfect crouch. But just as he was about to stand up, Ron flopped on top of him.

"Ow!" Ron cried, although he was glad Will had cushioned his fall.

Meanwhile, Killigan was raising a new club in the air. "No one can touch my short game!" he taunted.

But before he could finish his swing, Will charged right up to him. He pushed the button on his standard-issue GJN stopwatch and . . . *flub!*

It didn't work.

Killigan stared at the broken watch—then he looked at Will. "Are ya daft, man?"

Ron peeked over Will's shoulder and said, "Maybe you gotta set it for local time."

Killigan finished his swing, sending the explosive ball high over Kim's head.

This guy? A pro golfer? Kim thought. *Hardly!* "Ha! You missed!" she yelled.

But Killigan had the last laugh. "It's a wedge, lassie. It's got backspin!"

Sure enough, the ball was still moving. Spinning on the ground, it was reversing—and heading straight for Kim!

She tried to run, but she couldn't escape. *Kaboom!* The explosion sent her flying.

"Kim!" Ron cried out.

She landed on a patch of grass. Dirt from the explosion rained down on her. This golfer had pushed her way past peeved—Kim was in Utterly Upset City.

Then she saw something that made her smile. "Heh!" she said, looking at a stray dandelion.

Duff Killigan stood over her with an evil scowl on his face. "Oh, you're in trouble now, lassie."

"No, I'm not—you are," Kim said as she stood up.

"And how would that be?" Killigan asked with interest.

Kim bent down and plucked the dandelion. She waved it near his nose. "You've got dandelions."

Killigan sneered. "A wee weed. Bah!"

"Sure," said Kim, "but see every one of these little cottony things? They're seeds . . . every last one of them."

Killigan was sweating, his voice hesitant. "Aye. So?"

"So, make a wish," Kim said as she gently blew on the flower. The little cottony seeds formed a cloud around the mad golfer.

He stood there, confused and nervous. He went cross-eyed watching the one seed that landed on the tip of his nose.

Kim grabbed his watering can. *Splash!* She got him good.

"Aw, nah!" Killigan cried.

For a moment, nothing seemed to be happening. Then—*fump!*—the weeds completely grew over the golfer. One by one, white dandelions popped out, sprouting up faster than usual.

When Will and Ron ran over to join Kim, Duff Killigan had turned into *Fluff* Killigan—he was one big cottony ball of weed seeds. He looked more like a large sheep than an evil golfer.

"You're through now, lassie." Killigan spit seeds out as he babbled on. "Get these plants out of me mouthie!"

Kim crossed her arms and smiled. She asked Ron and Will, "Should we have him arrested or *mowed*?"

Kim was joking, but Agent Will Du didn't get it. "I'll have GJN send in a defoliation team."

"Or you could just give a neighborhood kid five bucks," Ron said.

"Humor. Amusing," Will said with a frown.

Rufus, on the other hand, was laughing his naked-mole-rat head off!

CHAPTER 10

NOW THAT DUFF KILLIGAN WAS TRAPPED AND AN EMERGENCY CLEANUP CREW HAD BEEN CALLED TO REMOVE THE GRASS AND ARREST HIM, KIM WANTED TO GET BACK TO THE BONNIE ROCKWALLER PROBLEM.

Saving the world from a rogue golfer? No big. But selling fund-raiser candy bars? That *was* a challenge.

She pushed Will toward his hover jet, which had just been uncovered. "Okay, bye. Got to get home and have another thorn removed from my side."

"Oooh!" A strange, spooky yell came from behind Kim. She turned to see Killigan leaping toward her.

Will snapped into position. He pushed the button on his stopwatch. This time it worked. *Zappo!* A shock ran through Killigan. He collapsed in a heap.

Will smiled. He had *finally* done something right!

Kim said, "Thanks. I've got to get one of those stopwatches."

Will lowered his head. For the first time, he wasn't acting like a brat. "Miss Possible, uh, Kimberly, I owe you . . . an apology."

"I'm glad you're a big enough person to admit it," Kim said, extending her hand.

Will grabbed Kim's hand and shook it. "You were of much assistance to me on this mission."

"Assistance?" Kim pulled her hand back. "Did you not pay attention to anything that happened?" she cried in disbelief.

"Farewell, Kim Possible." Once Agent Will Du had the last word, he was gone.

Kim stood there with her mouth open. "I do not believe that guy."

Ron walked over and listened to Kim spout off about Will. "He won't even consider that maybe somebody else deserves some credit," she said. "Maybe somebody else is as good as him."

"Maybe better," Ron said.

"Yes!" Kim was going full rant now.

Ron broke in. "We should get back to Middleton."

Kim kept going. "You know, how hard is it to admit that somebody else is doing a great job?"

Ron put his hands on his friend's shoulder. "Seriously, Kim. We've gotta get back. You've got that whole Bonnie thing."

"Oh, and Bonnie—when will she just *give it up*?" Kim cried. "The fund-raising, the uniforms, the new routine . . ."

"KP?" Ron interrupted.

"You're right, Ron. We've gotta go."

Back home, in the Middleton High gym, Bonnie Rockwaller stood in front of the other members of the Martial Arts Club. All the members were there—well, all but one.

"Uh, I really think we should wait for Kim before we decide who's gonna be co-captain," Tara told Bonnie.

Bonnie threw a fit. "She's gonna be, like, forever. I want this captain thing decided *now.*"

Just then, Kim and Ron walked into the gym. Kim wore her new uniform—the one that Bonnie had helped the team buy. "Relax, Bonnie," she said. "I'm back."

"Thank goodness," Tara sighed with relief.

"Let's do it," Bonnie hissed.

"Fine by me." Kim turned to her teammates. The whole way back from Japan, Kim had thought about what she would say to them.

She had thought about Will Du. He had wanted to be the number one agent so much that he refused to give Kim any credit. And the mission was almost a big zero because of it.

Unless she wanted to act just like Will, Kim knew what she had to do. She took a deep breath and said, "I vote for Bonnie as the new captain."

The Martial Arts Club members gasped! Bonnie was the most surprised of all. "You do? But I don't even know anything about martial arts," Bonnie added.

"Well," said Kim, "most of us here know about martial arts, it being the Martial Arts Club and all. But as co-captain, your fund-raising, the awesome uniforms, and that new combat sequence . . . I've gotta admit: you would be the perfect co-captain."

"Are you serious?" Bonnie couldn't believe it.

Kim nodded, then asked in a big voice, "So, all in favor of Bonnie?"

Everyone responded with shouts of "Yay, Bonnie!" and "You go, girl!"

The Martial Arts Club had found a new co-captain.

Kim congratulated Bonnie with a pat on the back. "You really worked hard for this."

"Yes," Bonnie said with an exhausted shrug of her shoulders. "Glad that's over."

"Bonnie, you're the co-captain now," Kim said. "You *do* realize that the hard work is just beginning?"

A look of horror crossed Bonnie's face. "You're kidding, right?" Her voice cracked.

Kim smiled. "You know, suddenly I couldn't be happier for you."

As Bonnie sulked out of the gym, Ron snapped her a salute. "Cap'n Bonnie!"

She ignored him. She was too busy thinking about what Kim had told her.

"I've gotta *keep* working hard and learn," she groaned. "This is *so* unfair."

Ron whispered to Kim, "You countin' on the fact that she'll only last a month?"

Kim winked at her best friend. "I give her two weeks—tops."

MIDDLETON TRIBUNE

Caught in the Middle of Current Events

MIDDLETON TEEN SAVES TOKYO

This week, Kim Possible traveled to multiple international destinations to stop a greedy golf enthusiast named Duff Killigan. After retired professor Sylvan Green went missing from his Florida retirement home, Possible was recruited by the Global Justice Network, or GJN, to find the missing professor.

But this wasn't a solo mission. Possible teamed up with GJN's top agent, Will Du, who is definitely a good student, to locate Professor Green and quell any possible global threat.

After meeting at the underground headquarters of the GJN, Du and Possible headed out to Killigan's secret island lair off the coast of a country we can only assume to be Scotland, given the excessive amount of plaid Killigan typically sports. After expertly escaping a quicksand trap, the team headed straight for Tokyo, where Killigan had already begun his maniacal grass-invasion spree.

Possible deflected exploding golf balls until she noticed a weed growing among the grass. A well-planted blow (of dandelion seeds) struck Killigan, and thanks to Possible's crime-fighting skills, she was able to hand off Killigan to local GJN authorities. One thing is *fore* sure, this rogue golfer won't be hitting the greens anytime soon.

Fill these pages with top secret notes and details about your next high-tech mission!